Tessa wasn't looking forward to going back to her old home town and meeting Paul Mellor again—she had made a fool of herself over Paul once before and didn't want to repeat the experience. But was Orme Jared's solution to her problem likely to be the right one?

FOUR WEEKS IN WINTER

BY

JANE DONNELLY

MILLS & BOON LIMITED
17–19 FOLEY STREET
LONDON W1A 1DR

First published *1977*
Philippine copyright *1977*
This edition *1977*

© Jane Donnelly 1977

ISBN 0 263 72481 6

Set in Baskerville 11 pt.

Made and printed in Great Britain by
Richard Clay (The Chaucer Press), Ltd., Bungay, Suffolk

CHAPTER ONE

TESSA HARRIS stood for a few minutes looking into the antique shop window, her eyes fixed on the tray of rings. It was pretty Victorian jewellery, moderately priced, and after a quick glance up and down the road, as though checking for someone who might recognise her on the crowded streets, she slipped into the shop.

The middle-aged man with a goatee beard, who looked as though he could have done with a dust-down as well as some of his shelves, ambled forward prepared to hear the usual 'Just looking around', but the girl said, 'The tray of rings in the window —could I see them, please?'

He leaned through the gap in the red velvet curtains and lifted out the tray, edging it precariously over china bric-à-brac, and placed it on a table.

Tessa picked out a little blue heart in turquoise chips and tried it on the third finger of her right hand, but it slipped around, at least a size too big. She had thin hands, with short pink polished nails. She wore no rings but a slim digital watch on her wrist, and the rings she was looking at now seemed an odd choice for her, as though modern jewellery would have been more her style.

She was dressed in fashion. Not blatantly so, but she knew what suited her. She was small, almost skinny, but the general effect was vital and attractive. She wouldn't be overlooked. She was a girl on the move, who knew where she was going. A girl of today, now poring over a tray of rings from another century.

She picked out another one quickly. This time it was a row of seed pearls, and this time it fitted. 'Yes, please,' she said.

'Anything else?' the shop owner suggested. 'I could show you a bracelet that would go nicely with this.'

'Not just now.' Her smile was wide and warm, and her clean fresh perfume cleared a little of the mustiness from the small cluttered shop. 'Another time, perhaps,' she said.

'Will you be wearing it?'

'No.'

He put it into a ring box, into a bag, and Tessa paid and took her purchase, dropping it into her handbag before she came out of the shop and stood for a split second in the doorway, glancing up and down the street.

It was crazy to feel guilty. She was doing nothing that could affect anyone but herself, and if she should walk slap bang into one of her colleagues there was no reason why she shouldn't be coming out of an antique shop. Skulking like a fugitive from Special Branch was just plain silly.

She stepped into the street and walked fast. Her dark brown hair, brushed back from her forehead, waved naturally and flipped up at the ends, shone when the sun caught it. Her eyes were the same brown, sherry-flecked, and although she was no great beauty glances followed her.

There was still half an hour of her lunch hour to spare, but she wasn't hungry. She hadn't been hungry for several days. She spent the rest of her time window-shopping, staring at displays behind plate glass but seeing very little. When she glimpsed her own reflection she was surprised how composed she looked.

6

That was some comfort. Nobody would guess how she felt. Not now, nor tomorrow, please God. But when she thought about tomorrow a flutter of panic rose in her throat, and when she tried to swallow she almost choked.

It had to be lived through, there was no way out of that, and with her lunch hour over she turned back again to the office.

Tessa was a TV research girl. She loved the work and she did it well. She had joined the company as a secretary, watching and weighing the opportunities. and now—at twenty-two—she was part of a current-events documentary team, second to none.

That wasn't just her opinion either. They scooped the awards. Orme Jared, producer-director, was a name to conjure with, and she enjoyed almost every minute of her working day. Some of her nights were spent working too. The hours in this business were erratic.

But she was lucky to have the job. Maybe she had been due for a break, but suddenly it had come. She had been sent up to do some secretarial work for Jared and gone a little nervously; he had a reputation for expecting miracles. She knew him by sight, of course, a big man, usually moving fast, and that was how he dictated.

She got the dictation down. She would have done in any case, she had good shorthand speeds, but right from the beginning there had been something about Orme Jared that got her adrenalin flowing. Even now she wasn't sure whether she liked him or loathed him, but wherever he was things happened, the atmosphere crackled. That was why the awards came. The men who worked with him were a brilliant team, but it was Jared's master touch that made his programmes small masterpieces.

That day, just over a year ago, there had been a point of query, in the assessment of a possible programme that he was dictating, and Tessa had offered, 'I'll check, shall I?'

A phone had rung, and as she answered it he had nodded at her, and she had raced to do the checking. Then out of the blue she had found herself being taken on a month's trial as secretary, research girl, and general dogsbody.

That wasn't how things were usually done. Most researchers had university degrees, but Orme Jared must have decided she had something to contribute to the team. He usually backed his own judgment, and his judgment was sound, because Tessa was bright and prepared to work herself into the ground.

Perhaps that was what he was looking for. Until she began to work for him she hadn't realised how much could be crammed into an hour.

'How are you getting on?' someone asked her during that first week, and Tessa, belting along the corridor, only had time to gasp, 'He's working me to skin and bones!'

When he addressed her as 'Our Miss Bones' she knew that he had heard about that and for a moment she was embarrassed. Then he grinned, and from then on she had a pet name, 'Bones'. A new job, a new name, a new life. From then on things had gone wonderfully well for her.

Her glow of confidence came from being part of the Jared team. Her colleagues and their families were her closest friends, almost her family.

She did have a social life, outside her work. She made friends easily, but dates had to accept last-minute cancellations and wait patiently while she went off filming in Teheran. Not many men would, which meant that she had plenty of boy-friends and

8

was deeply involved with none of them.

Her real life was her job. Just as her real friends were the team she worked and travelled with, but if she had tried to explain to them what was worrying her now they would have laughed at her. They were a grand bunch, but they would never understand how shaken she was at the prospect of going back to that small town where she was born.

She had left it when she was eighteen, early, one bitterly cold morning, promising herself this was a journey of no return. She had kept in touch for a while with some of the people she had known all her life, but five years is a long time, and they were down to Christmas cards now with brief notes scrawled on them.

When she got her job with the Jared team she had been tempted to write and tell somebody that Tessa Harris's career was coming along nicely, or to send postcards from one of the more exotic places to which her work took her.

But she hadn't.

There were things that were best left undisturbed, to die quietly and naturally. So it had come as a nasty shock to hear that Blackstone was a place on which they would be descending in the near future.

Orme had the theme of a programme mapped out, and executive approval, when he presented the team with it.

They all shared an office on the fourth floor of a massive glass and concrete building, with Orme Jared's name on the door, and his big desk—with the window behind him—and desks and tables and filing cabinets standing around.

When Tessa first entered this room she had thought it looked chaotic and disorganised, but she

9

soon learned there was nothing slipshod about these men and it would be more than her job was worth to start tidying up for them. So she kept her own area clear, her papers in her drawers, and left everything else well alone.

'There's this coalmine in the Midlands,' Orme had said. 'It's shut down, but for nearly a hundred years it dominated the town. It had rather a hairy reputation, and one major disaster—fifty years ago—has almost become a local legend. We're going down to look up some of the men who worked there and find out what's happened to them, to talk to anybody who has any memories of the disaster. Rehash the history.'

'Where is it?' Freddie Behague had asked. Freddie was their sound recordist, a gangling figure in his early thirties, with mild blue eyes and bushy hair that sprang out like a halo in a high wind. The immovable thing on his desk was a photograph of his wife Joy, and the twins Gina and Gareth. Tessa loved the twins, they called her Auntie Bones.

'Blackstone, in Staffordshire,' Orme had said, and Tessa's dread was realised, because Blackstone was the small town she had never wanted to see again.

'The Grey Lady pit,' said Orme.

'The Lady is a killer,' said Tessa softly, and Orme said,

'You read too many thrillers.'

She twiddled a pencil between her fingers, looking at it not at him, telling them all, 'That's a local saying. I should know. My father worked in the Lady pit until it closed.'

They knew that she had no family now. They knew her father had been a jobbing gardener when he died, when she was seventeen. He had only been sixty, but Tessa remembered him as an old man. All her life he seemed to have been an old man.

This was the first time she had named her home town, and it seemed a happy coincidence. Her main task was fixer. She dug up facts, but she also arranged things, organising ahead so that the team had a draft schedule ready before they started; and as she knew the town, and some of the folk who lived there, she had to be starting with an advantage.

In theory she was. She knew names she could call on, where she should get co-operation, but her stomach was churning and she was wondering if she could fall sick, if there was any excuse that could keep her away from Blackstone while they were making this film.

Fine, they were all saying, there's a bit of luck. There were three of them besides Orme and Tessa: Freddie; Spike Morgan, photographer, small, wiry and dark, married, and an artist with a camera; and reporter James Catling.

Only Orme was eyeing her inquiringly. Sitting back in the swivel-chair he was impressive even when he was saying nothing. His size had something to do with that. He was tall and built powerfully. He had a big nose and heavy brows, and the shoulders of a blacksmith.

Rugged would have been the word for him, except that his voice was cultured and his clothes were impeccably cut. His grandfather had been an admiral and his grandmother was the daughter of an earl. He had all the advantages of a privileged background, but they didn't come any more down to earth, nor harder to fool, and he was the one asking, 'What's the catch?'

'C-catch?' Tessa had stammered.

'No joy going home?'

She hadn't been exactly beaming, but she didn't

think she could have looked as shocked as she felt and she said quickly, 'It's years since I was there, but it should be fun to see what's happened to the place and look up some old friends.'

That piece of hypocrisy stuck in her throat. 'Good,' said Orme. 'Then get on with it.'

Tessa usually went ahead of them, getting her facts on the spot, but this time she used the phone as much as she could. She booked lodgings. She contacted the Coal Board authorities and enlisted the help of the editor of the local newspaper. She got a list of names of the men who had worked at the Lady and were possibly still around locally. Harris wasn't an unusual name. She had spoken to no one who remembered her, or associated her with Arnold Harris, whose name was on her list; and it was possible that she could live and work in Blackstone for the next three weeks and no one would spot her. But it wasn't likely. A TV team was going to attract everyone's attention. She was bound to be recognised.

The last piece of filming was finished, the team had nothing to keep them here in head office, so tomorrow they were all going down together, Tessa and Orme in Orme's car, with Spike and his wife who had no children and who travelled around with Spike as much as she could. Freddie and Jimmy and the equipment had a Ford Escort van.

Tessa was in the lift alone after lunch, going up to the fourth floor, and she took the ring out of its box and put it on her left hand, her engagement finger. It didn't look much, perhaps she should have bought something more spectacular, like a big flashy phoney diamond. But it was too late now. It would have to be an heirloom, something of sentimental value.

'Where the blazes have you been?' demanded

Orme the moment she stepped through the door.

She was not late. 'I've been to lunch,' she began, but there was a flap on, and some of it was Tessa's fault. She had had things on her mind this morning, besides her work, and she had slipped a report she had typed into her own drawer instead of into Orme's tray. It was right on top of the drawer, if he'd looked for it he could have found it, but he preferred to bellow, and the rest of the afternoon seemed to pass even more hectically than usual.

It was six o'clock before she had time to draw breath and sit back. They were all going home now, to make for the Stag's Head in Blackstone tomorrow. No one had even noticed her ring. A girl would have done, but to a man it was just a ring. That meant she would have to point it out tomorrow. She would show it to Spike's Annie, and break the news that way.

She was weary tonight. The prospect of Blackstone was wearing and it had been a very busy day. She nearly nodded off in the bus that took her from the TV centre to her home, a flat in a block of ten flats where one Edwardian house once stood.

When she first came here Tessa had lived in a hostel, then with a succession of girls in a succession of bed-sits. She had had fun along the way, but she preferred this place which was her very own.

She had furnished it carefully, some new furniture, some near antique, selecting pieces that she enjoyed living with. It was one of the perks of success because, in a small way, she was successful.

She didn't have a date tonight. Six weeks ago she had met Derek, waiting for a taxi in the rain when she had just washed her hair. They had shared the taxi and he had left with her phone number, ringing the office the next day.

But he was reaching the stage where he was getting awkward about her job. At first he had found it interesting, but she had let him down once or twice, working, and he was beginning to protest. Now she would be away for three weeks, and any minute he was going to issue an ultimatum—him or the job. That had happened before. It usually did, and when it did it would be goodbye to Derek.

She had her case packed. Everything was ready, and she was facing the scraps from the fridge that could be her evening meal—some wholemeal biscuits with two sausages, three salami rings, some cottage cheese, one egg and a carton of yogurt—when the door bell rang.

She opened the door on the chain and stood blinking. Then she asked, 'Whatever's happened?'

Orme Jared had never called on her in an evening before. He had phoned sometimes, always about work; and tomorrow his Daimler would be raising the tone of the neighbourhood long enough for Tessa to run downstairs and clamber aboard.

It never occurred to her that this might be a social call. She was sure that something had been mislaid, or a hitch had developed around the colliery story. She took off the chain and held back the door, and he walked through.

This was not the first time he had seen her home. She usually travelled in his car and he sometimes collected her, but she was always ready to go. Keeping Orme Jared waiting was not on; patience was not among his virtues.

He was wearing a camel overcoat over a brown suit of fine hopsack tweed, cream silk shirt, brown silk tie. His shoes were handmade, at least she presumed they were. He always dressed immaculately and conservatively, which was flying false colours

14

when the man inside the suit made his own rules and went his own way. Like the manicured nails on the strong hands. She had seen him lift the back of a car from a muddy verge, that Jimmy and Spike couldn't manage between them. He was powerful. He took power for granted and although Tessa admired him tremendously professionally, and wouldn't have wanted to work for anyone else, she was never quite at ease in his company.

He was less tolerant than the others. They spoiled her a little. Spike's and Freddie's wives got on well with her, there was no jealousy, and Jimmy the un-attached treated her like a kid sister. But Orme gave her no leeway at all.

He bawled her out, as he bawled anyone who, in his opinion, was being stupid or inefficient or a plain and simple nuisance. She got support and she got appreciation from him, but that was because she always put her job first. If she hadn't she was sure he would have fired her without a qualm.

His team would have followed him through quicksands, and professionally Tessa supposed she would have gone along too, but there had always been a hint of antagonism in her feelings for Orme. Not that it surfaced often. She wasn't likely to tell him, 'There are times when I think your name should have been juggernaut, not Jared,' but oc-casionally she flared a little and was put down with infuriating promptness.

Now he stood in the middle of her living room, on the red and blue Spanish rug, looking across at the Lowry print 'Outside the Mill' on the wall, and she heard herself say defensively, 'You don't expect the real thing on my salary, do you?'

He had a Georgian town house, and all his pic-tures were the real thing. 'Are you complaining

15

about your salary?' he asked, and of course she wasn't. She had only said that because he made her nervous, standing there.

'I'm not complaining at all,' she said. 'I'm just jittery that something's gone wrong.'

'Like what?'

'That's what I'm waiting to hear. Why you're here. It is trouble, isn't it?'

'May I sit down?'

He seated himself in her two-seater settee, which was a better fit than her straight-backed stripped-pine chairs would have been, while she was still frowning apprehensively. 'Please do,' she said, several seconds too late.

'There's something I want to discuss with you,' he said, and she gulped in a soundless breath of dismay. Something that had to be said in privacy must be grim, and the worst thing that could happen to her would be if he told her she was being made redundant. They were doing well, every programme they produced was a winner, but perhaps somebody had decided she wasn't needed on the team any more. Or perhaps she had made some dreadful mistake that had only just come to light.

Only work would bring Orme here, and she was so convinced he was going to say something horrible that when he said, 'That ring you're wearing,' she could only croak:

'What?'

'Your ring.'

There was the note of exasperation in his voice that meant she was being slow on the uptake, and she gulped and said 'What about it?'

'Is it an engagement ring?'

So somebody had noticed. So why hadn't he said anything when he'd noticed? Probably because they had been so busy this afternoon, and that would have interrupted the working tempo. 'As a matter of fact,' she said airily, 'it is.'

'Congratulations.'

'Thank you.' She couldn't believe he had come all this way just to congratulate her on getting engaged.

'When are you getting married?' he asked.

'We haven't set a date.' That bit was true. If any of the others had asked her she could have smiled, and looked happy and bashful like a girl who has just got engaged, but with Orme sitting there, firing the questions, she felt like somebody under attack.

She offered desperately, 'Will you have a coffee, or a drink?'

The table looked downright sluttish, with leftovers still in packages and the yogurt in its cardboard container. Tessa wished she had laid it nicely, and been sitting here at an elegant small repast. Of course it didn't really matter, but she explained, 'I'm eating up the leftovers and emptying the fridge.'

'You'll make a thrifty housewife,' he said.

He didn't make that sound like a compliment, and she offered again, 'Can I get you a drink?'

'What do you have?'

'Not much.' If he was going to be selective almost nothing. A bottle of plonk that he would consider undrinkable, and the dregs of some whisky she had bought for Derek. Both Derek and the bottle of whisky were near the end of their tether. She opened the corner cupboard and suggested, 'Whisky?'

Orme came up behind her, bending down to take out the two bottles, replacing the whisky bottle with its inch of amber liquid. 'I don't drink alone,' he said.

'You don't?' Tessa looked up, kneeling, and he asked,

'Did you think I did?'

17

She couldn't imagine Orme Jared having sorrows to drown, nor needing the secret stimulus of alcohol. 'No,' she said. 'But I don't want——' she began, and he raised a heavy eyebrow.

'I should have expected you to be celebrating.'

It did look odd, her being alone tonight of all nights. She didn't even want a glass of wine with Orme in case it loosened her tongue, but that sounded so inhospitable that she hurried to find a corkscrew and a couple of glasses.

While he opened the bottle Tessa moved things around on the table, as though putting the scraps into a pattern would turn them into a buffet. It gave her something to do, she was twitching with nervousness. She knew that he was going to cross-question her, and even with him over the other side of the room she was as conscious of him as though his hands were on her shoulders.

The cork came out smoothly, and he sat down again on the settee to pour out the two glasses. She walked over to take the glass he was holding up for her, and then she seated herself very carefully on a chair, hoping her hands wouldn't shake.

'I don't know what you're going to think about this,' she began to babble. 'The wine, I mean. If I'd known you were coming I'd have got a decent bottle, but you can put this in stews as well as drink it, so it's a bargain at the price.'

'Where is he?' Orme asked.

'Out of town,' she said promptly.

'Who is he?'

She drank some of her wine. 'No one you know.'

'Not Derek what's-his-name?'

Derek had been the one who'd phoned her most at the office in the past few weeks, although there had been others, she was not dating Derek exclusively; and she hadn't realised that Orme knew her dates by name.

But they did say there was nothing that got by him, and that she believed. If she had known he was going to want details like this she would have thought again about starting it.

'So what is his name?' he asked.

'John Reynolds.'

'What does he do?'

These were hard and fast questions and answers, not friendly interest. He knew something was wrong, and he would catch her out if he could. 'He's a vet,' she said.

'Where?'

'In Yorkshire.'

'How long have you known him?'

'Not very long.' If she said 'Ages' they'd wonder why she'd never mentioned him before.

'Are you pregnant?' He still spoke in the same dry impersonal voice, and her cheeks burned with indignation. It was a wonder she hadn't sent her glass of wine splashing all over.

'*No!*'

'Sorry to shock you, but this does seem to be rather an abrupt decision and I need to know if you're planning to leave us soon.'

'I'm not.' Tessa felt as though her whole body was blushing, her tongue stuck to the roof of her mouth, and she wished she could have screamed her outrage at him.

'Good,' he said, and he took a few sips of wine before he added, 'I apologise if I offended you.'

Of course he had offended her, although these days some people thought that pregancy was the only good reason for marriage, and this engagement of hers was sudden and unexpected. She said coldly,

'If I was it would be none of your business.'

'Professionally it would,' said Orme. 'You must see that.'

It was a real effort to admit, 'I suppose so,' and she did it grudgingly.

'So you fell in love,' he said. 'A bolt from the blue.'

'It can happen like that.' But that wasn't how it had happened to her. It had grown with her, over the years. Love with all its bright dreams and its terrible desolate aftermath. Love was a painful thing and she wanted no more of it.

'Mr Right the vet from Yorkshire.' Orme was smiling at her now. 'He sounds quite a character.'

'He is.'

'Tell me about him.'

'You wouldn't find him interesting. He's very ordinary by your standards, and I don't think I want this wine. It's going to be a long day tomorrow, isn't it? I'll need a clear head.'

'Yes.' He looked straight at her, then he said very softly, 'Why don't you want to go back?'

How did he know that? She pulled an astonished face. 'What *do* you mean?'

'Drink your wine,' he said. 'They say the human race is born two drinks below par.'

'Who says?'

'The brewers, probably. What are you doing, Bones? What's going on?'

Tessa began to laugh, not making a very convincing job of it. 'What on earth are you talking about?' she said, and Orme told her:

'When I said we were going to Blackstone you shut your eyes. What were you shutting out?'

'*Nothing*. I must have blinked.'

'Were you happy there?'

'Happy enough.'

'But you've never been back?'

She had told them all it was years since she had been in Blackstone, and she took a drink now to give herself the courage to say, 'Stop questioning me like this. What's it for? What do you want?'

'I want you to tell me if you need any help,' he said.

There were limits to what even Orme could do, but if she had been in tangible trouble there was no one whose support she would rather have had. She said, 'Thank you,' before she realised she should be denying her need. Then she said, 'I didn't leave under a cloud. Nobody's going to make things awkward for us when I go back. You don't need to worry about that.'

'Fair enough.' He took her almost empty glass and filled it again. 'We'll leave Blackstone till we get there. Now I want you to drink this and I want to hear about this man you're going to marry.'

Perhaps she was stupid to drink any more, but Orme standing over her was not to be denied. She gulped obediently, 'Are you getting me drunk?'

'Just talking. I'm not leaving here until I know what's going on.'

Two glasses of wine would hardly act as a truth drug, and there wasn't much to tell that he wasn't working out for himself. He didn't sit down again. He went across to the table and took a biscuit. 'No butter?' he said.

'Sorry, I'm out of it. How about some cottage cheese?'

'I'm not a cottage cheese man,' and he smiled across at her. 'Feeling more relaxed?'

'I feel fine.' She was supposed to be a girl who had just got engaged. She should have been on top of the world; of course she wasn't, but she had been doubly tense since he'd walked in. He knew how she felt. He was going to make her talk, because she was part of his team and things were not right with her, and when she did he would think she was a complete idiot.

She said miserably, 'I do wish you'd leave me alone. This will sound so ridiculous to everybody.'

'You're not telling everybody, you're telling me.' He was still over by the table, and she stayed in her chair, turned away from him.

'All right,' she said. 'I'm not looking forward to going back . . .'

Five years should have made her invulnerable, but beneath all the layers of living the memory was still there, as savage as though it had happened yesterday.

She had always hero-worshipped Paul Mellor. From when she was a skinny child, living in one of the cottages backing on to the churchyard and the moors, and he sometimes rode over the hills on a beautiful horse. She had thought he was some sort of prince then, and as far as she was concerned he might have been, he was that far out of her reach. Although he was in fact the son of the town's leading lawyer, eight years older than Tessa and moving in quite another social stratum.

After her mother died she had kept house for her father, although she was still at school. When she left school she took a job in the office at a small supermarket. She dreamed of moving into Paul's office, he was qualified by then in his father's firm, and dreams were the nearest she got to living life to the full. She didn't get out much, she had very little spare time, and the nearest she got to Paul Mellor was that her father did a couple of days a week in the Mellor gardens after the pit closed down.

Paul Mellor certainly never gave her a second thought. She was Harris's daughter, around sometimes when he was working, and that was all she was. When Harris died the family was kind to her at the funeral, and Mrs Mellor inquired if there was anything they could do, and stressed that Tessa must always think of them as her friends.

Mrs Mellor called at the cottage one evening the following week to say that all over again. She kissed Tessa and said, 'Now you know where we are, my dear, any time at all,' and went away in a charitable glow.

Three months later Paul Mellor bumped into Tessa in the high street and greeted her with, 'Well, if it isn't Tessa, how's my favourite girl?' Her peony-pink blush amused and flattered him. She was becoming attractive. There was a promise of something out of the ordinary run about her, and she was looking at him with undisguised delight.

That evening he took her along to a party. The hosts and the guests all lived nearby, but Tessa had never met any of them socially before, and she would have been speechless with shyness if Paul hadn't brought her.

That was the magic key that unlocked the golden gates. Paul had asked her to come with him, and she was Cinderella at the ball, transformed from drabness into bright and glittering beauty.

Looking back she could see what a mirage the months that followed had been, but at the time they had been real to her and she had thought they would last for ever. Paul's feelings were a brief infatuation, but she had worshipped him. The days she didn't see him were empty and then she would write to him, telling him everything, her dreams, her hopes, everything.

She had always had a gift for words, English had

been her best subject, and she wrote love letters for Paul, and as he tired of Tessa he showed her letters around so that, in the end, she knew they must all have been laughing at her.

One particularly bitchy girl—although she might have been the kindest of the lot—told Tessa what was going on, and that Paul was going to marry Stella Spencer one day and everybody knew it.

She could have disintegrated with a display of public hysteria, but instead she drew back and watched and it was true. Next day she said she was going to London and saw the relief in Paul's eyes . . .

Now she said, 'There was a man there. There still is. The affair went sour. I was the loser and everybody knew I was making myself a laughing stock.'

Orme came across, picked up her hand from her lap, holding her ring. 'What's this, then?'

'It's temporary. Just while I'm down there.'

He put her hand back on her lap and she thought —he'll start laughing in a minute. He'll tell me I must be out of my tiny mind. 'The vet from Yorkshire must be very obliging,' he said.

'You know darn well there's no vet from Yorkshire. I made him up.'

'Why? You don't need the status symbol of a ring on your finger. They'll only have to look at you to know you stopped being a loser a long time ago.'

She supposed she had. There were only achievers on his team. 'So take it off,' he said.

When she made no move he took her hand again, but she clenched her fingers and whispered, 'No, please, I——' It would have been hard to explain to anybody, it was almost impossible to explain to him. She said, 'You're going to laugh at me,' and she bit her lip in a mockery of a smile.

'No one is laughing,' he said, 'and no one is going to hear any of this. I give you my word.'

He held her hand still, but Tessa closed her eyes because she couldn't look at him while she told him. With closed eyes, dark lashes on her pale cheeks, she said, 'I'm scared. Of course I'm not in love with Paul now, but I do know that I'm more—attractive than I was. Men want me now—some men. Paul might, and if he did I don't know how I should react.

'As long as I can remember I thought Paul was so wonderful. I grew up nearly worshipping him, and even now when I see somebody who looks like him I can still feel cut up. Not that I see many who look like him. He was—like a Greek god, he even had golden hair.' She sensed Orme's impatience and shrank back, her eyes still closed, her head bowed.

'So this morning I thought if I put on a ring and told you all I was engaged that would show I wasn't available. It would be a protection. I like my life the way it is. I don't want to get involved with Paul again. It would be the most destructive thing that could happen to me, and an engagement ring is a Keep Off sign, isn't it?'

Orme loosed her hand as she opened her eyes, and said, 'You wouldn't have got away with it. No letters from Yorkshire, no phone calls, no fiancé turning up at the Stag's Head to check the competition.'

She would have found it difficult, but that only showed how desperate she was. She hadn't thought of the snags, only of protecting herself. 'You're right,' she said at last.

'On the other hand, we don't want you with your mind on Greek gods instead of on the film.' He grinned, but he wasn't laughing at her, and she managed a smile.

'I know it's stupid.' She took off the ring. 'I'm sorry. I won't make a fool of myself.'

'That you won't,' said Orme. 'Not while you're

working for me. But if you think it would help we'll put a Keep Off sign on you.'

'How?'

He went across to another print on the wall, this one was an abstract of swirling colours, and straightened it a fraction, standing back to check. 'An engagement ring,' he said, 'from a very possessive man, right there on the spot.'

Tessa had been getting up from her seat, but at that she sagged back again. 'Who?' she croaked.

'Me, of course,' he said.

CHAPTER TWO

'You're joking, of course,' said Tessa.

'Not in the least.' Orme turned from the picture he had just straightened on the wall. 'Can you suggest a better Keep Off sign than me?'

His kind of dynamism made a dangerous aura. He would only have to loom up to scare off ninety-nine men in a hundred, and Tessa's lips twitched. She was going to start giggling hysterically because this was hysterically funny. 'Frankly no,' she said in a shaking voice, 'but of course nobody's going to believe it.'

'No?' He sounded surprised.

'Well,' she pointed first at him and then at herself, 'you, me, they'll know it's a con and then they'll wonder why.' She meant the men who worked with them and who knew them well. 'I don't want anyone else to know about Paul,' she said. 'It's so stupid to think that after all these years I might still make a fool of myself over a man who——'

'Who could prove the most destructive thing that could happen to you, I think you said.' Orme's deep voice overran her faltering and that was what she had said, it was the risk she ran. It stilled the laughter in her and he went on, very quietly, 'You're doing well, Bones. You're good, you can make it, you've a great future ahead of you. I don't want to see you dragged back. Do you?'

He had never said this to her before, although she had never needed reassurance before like she did today. Such praise from him was a tremendous confidence-booster. Of course she wanted that future. Loving Paul had only brought hurt that she could remember still.

'No,' she said, 'or I'd hardly have tried this charade, would I?' She held the ring in the palm of her hand, and she looked at it now.

'So while we're in Blackstone,' said Orme, 'I'm the man in your life.'

Most of the time he was the man in charge anyway, almost the man in possession. But only professionally. Her links with him were less personal than with any of the others in the team.

'You can call it off as soon as we get back,' he was saying, 'and because we're civilised folk we shall stay good friends.'

He was smiling, and really he had to be joking. Again the giggles rose in her. 'Nobody is going to believe it,' she said.

'Why not?' He sat down again on the settee, long legs outstretched. 'I'm generally considered a fairly eligible bachelor.'

He was more than eligible. He was unmarried in his mid-thirties entirely by his own choice. There was always some gorgeous female phoning up Orme. He moved around with the best of them, but Tessa was sure he hadn't asked any of them to marry him, because if he had done they would have done.

The wine had certainly relaxed her, dissolving her restraint, and now she had told Orme about Paul that was a relief in a way.

She said gaily, 'Oh, you're eligible enough, look what you've got going for you. It's me.' Mischievously she added, 'Who's going to believe you asked me instead of Anthea Vella?'

Miss Vella was beautiful and rich, the daughter of a merchant banker and, by all accounts, Orme

Jared's current lady. But he didn't seem to be bothering what Miss Vella might make of this.

Tessa knew he wouldn't betray a confidence. It would have been the obvious thing, if he was serious about protecting Tessa from herself by standing between her and possible trouble, to explain the arrangement to Miss Vella. To make her promise to keep the secret but to tell her.

He wouldn't, though. He had given his word and he would keep it. Nothing Tessa had told him would go beyond these four walls. She had never been absolutely sure that she really liked Orme, but she had always been sure of his integrity.

'Don't underrate yourself,' he said cheerfully. 'They'll believe it.'

This was like playing a game. She was feeling lightheaded, as though she was at a party. She shook her head, producing the flaws quite triumphantly. 'No, they won't. No chance. They know what our relationship is. They know we've never even been out on a date together. Not just the two of us.'

'We'll tell them it was a bolt from the blue. You said yourself that could happen.'

'Did I?' A bolt from the blue, causing Orme to fall for her? No chance of that either. She was playing with the little ring, when somehow it slipped through her fingers, rolling on to the rug between them, and he stooped to pick it up.

'It's pretty,' he said, 'but——' But not what she would be wearing if she was engaged to him. A different type of ring would be required to back up that announcement.

'I was going to say it had sentimental value,' she told him, her voice blurring slightly in her ears. 'Actually I bought it at lunchtime. I only got the idea this morning.'

'Well, it's too late to get anything else now.' He handed it over to her and she stretched across an open palm, closing her fingers on the ring. 'Although I don't know,' he said suddenly. He stood up and ordered, 'Get your coat on.'

She opened very wide eyes. 'You're not going to get a ring?'

'There might be one around.'

Tessa knew she was a little fuzzy, but this was becoming wilder. 'An engagement ring?' she shrilled. 'You keep engagement rings around?'

'Not exactly.' As she made no move, except to stare with an open mouth at that puzzling reply, he said impatiently, 'Come on, girl,' and because she was so used to jumping to his commands she jumped up.

She swayed very slightly and he said, 'Are you all right?'

'Perfectly. Excuse me a moment.'

She went into her small bedroom, dropped the ring on the dressing table, and took a coat out of the wardrobe. It was a single-breasted grey simulated civet, her best coat; because although she had no idea where she was going her best coat seemed a good idea.

She would have liked to do things to her face, but the habit of not keeping Orme waiting was deeply ingrained. So she combed her hair quickly, gave herself a quick flick of lipstick, put on her coat and went straight back into the living room.

He didn't offer any further explanations. He was standing by the door into the corridor, and as Tessa came through the bedroom door he walked out of the flat. She followed and he waited for her to join him, so that they went downstairs together. But he said nothing, and neither did she.

She wondered how she was going to feel when she got out into the colder air. It could well hit with a sobering force, but even if it did she didn't know how she was going to stop what had started. This was Orme's scheme now, and it was very rarely indeed that anything stopped Orme.

One of the neighbours had popped out of a ground floor flat, and was watching the two of them coming downstairs. Mrs Prestcott was an old busybody, but Tessa quite liked her and always answered her questions goodhumouredly.

Now Mrs Prestcott said, 'Good evening,' with a dreadful archness.

'Good evening,' said Orme.

'Hello,' said Tessa.

Mrs Prestcott had seen Orme before, but never escorting Tessa on what looked like an evening date. Tessa glanced back, as they went out into the little cul-de-sac of the flats, and Mrs Prestcott was nodding and beaming like a mechanical toy. She seemed to approve of Orme. She knew who he was and she thought that Tessa had found herself a very distinguished escort.

If I come back with a suitable Jared-type engagement ring, thought Tessa, I'll show it her in the morning. But she changed her mind about that immediately, realising that when she had to explain that the engagement was off she could expect an inquest lasting for weeks.

She was into the cushioning luxury of the car before the chilly wind had time to reach anything but her face, and she sank back in her seat as Orme started up the engine, backed and turned them on to the road.

She was beginning to wish now that she hadn't had to tell him about Paul. She felt quite squeamish when she thought about that, a physical nausea under the euphoria of the wine and the exhilaration of what Orme had said about her doing well at her job. 'You can make it,' he'd said. 'You've a great future ahead.'

That was marvellous and this was a marvellous car, but Tessa didn't feel too good, not even when she put her head back. 'Where are we going?' she asked.

'To my place.' That was the other side of town. Give or take a few hold-ups that would be about half an hour, and she hoped she could make it. 'If Spike and Annie are home,' he said, 'we'll break the news to them.'

Spike and Annie had the top floor of Orme's house. It was three-storeyed, and Tessa had spent a lot of time in the top floor flat. She had been in Orme's rooms, but not on her own. She could never have dropped in on him, or invited herself round as she did with Spike and Annie.

She said, 'They won't believe it.'

'They'll be more likely to believe it than the phantom vet from Yorkshire,' said Orme.

'Want to bet?' She had her eyes closed by now, and her head was starting to ache a little. The car was still, at traffic lights, and she felt Orme shift in his seat, turning towards her, and knew he was looking closely at her.

'Were those two glasses of wine all you had?' he demanded.

'Yes,' she said. 'Mind you, I haven't eaten for days.'

'*What?*' The car moved smoothly away and she said,

'That's an exaggeration. But the thought of Blackstone has been taking the edge off my appetite lately, and today I missed my breakfast. Then I cut out lunch, and I was trying to work up an interest in the cottage cheese when you rang my bell.'

'That was a stupid thing to do, wasn't it?' He sounded exasperated with her and that wasn't fair.

'I would have eaten something if you hadn't turned up,' she retorted. 'And I wouldn't have drunk anything if you hadn't practically poured it down my throat.'

'All right,' he said, 'all right. You'd better shut up until you get some black coffee and some food inside you.'

After the third degree he'd just put her through that was typical of him. Tessa sighed deeply, but she kept quiet because she was in no state to argue. As soon as she had had something to eat, and was feeling more herself, then she would tell him again that the vet from Yorkshire—she really would have to remember his name, what *was* the name she'd invented?—anyhow, he was a better idea than asking anyone to believe that Orme was her lover.

Perhaps she wouldn't wear a ring after all. She was not available and she didn't need a ring to prove it. She would just remember what Orme had said, about her future with the team. Maybe she wouldn't even meet Paul again, and if she did come across him he might have no effect at all on her.

But she had never loved anyone else. After Paul there had always been an emotional wariness in her. She was very wary of Orme, because he was a very disturbing man. But there was no danger that he would ever ask anything from her, except that she stayed on top of her job, and nobody was going to believe that he had held her in his arms, and told her he loved her and asked her to marry him.

Not by the wildest leap of imagination could she

visualise that scene, although she had no doubt he was a compelling lover. She had often seen his charm in action, in public. In private, with Miss Vella and all the ladies who had gone before, he would know all the answers, all the ways, all there was to know, thought Tessa dourly.

She still wasn't hungry, but she knew that she ought to eat something, and it seemed that Orme was going to feed her. Then she would say, 'Please can we forget all this nonsense? I know I'll be all right, but if I look like making a fool of myself I'm sure you'll see, and then you can come down the heavy director, and that would make more sense than pretending you're my jealous lover.'

'Wake up,' said Orme abruptly. 'We're here.'

She had not been asleep. How could he expect her to fall asleep with all she had on her mind? Although this set-up was becoming rather like a dream, verging on a nightmare.

His house was in a row of Georgian houses, in a highly exclusive square. He opened the door with his key, and she followed him into the hall, with its dark green carpet and cool mint-green walls, and the slim white staircase that curved gracefully up to the first floor.

Spike and Annie usually used the back stairs, which went directly up to their flat. When she visited them so did Tessa, but tonight she was following Orme.

It was a beautiful house. Exquisite pieces of Chinese porcelain stood in small shell-topped alcoves, and at the top of the stairs was a genuine Turner. Orme's broad shoulders almost blotted out the view ahead, as she climbed the stairs behind him.

She had been in the drawing room, with its two

matching windows overlooking the street, and the old gilt-framed mirror between them. The mirror had a golden patina that took the harshness from all it reflected.

Tessa had come here to a Christmas party two months ago, and found the mirror so fascinating that she had stood looking into it for ages. Until she'd realised how odd that must appear, although it wasn't her own face so much as the whole company and the whole room in the mirror that enchanted her.

'Take your coat off,' said Orme, 'and I'll get you some food.'

She slipped out of her coat and put it on a chair. 'Thank you. Anything will do.'

'Which is what you'll get. It's Mrs Dacre's night off.'

He had a housekeeper, of course. Tessa sat on a small Victorian chair, covered in a pale-honey coloured satin, and thought this one wouldn't be much use to Orme, except possibly to put his feet up. She looked around for the chairs that would fit him, and from them selected a leather armchair in olive green on which her coat lay like a large slumbering cat as his possible favourite.

It was rather like waiting for the dentist. Not the surroundings, of course, but the growing apprehension, the hollowness and the threatening headache. Orme was back quickly and she didn't know whether she was glad or sorry to see him. He didn't make her feel less apprehensive, but the sooner she ate the sooner things should get straightened out.

He carried a tray with fruit, a pie in a dish, bread rolls and a butter dish. There was a large cup of black coffee, and he put down the tray on a side table and picked up the coffee. She had jumped up as soon as he came in, and he handed her the coffee.

'It's instant,' he said. 'You can have a decent cup later, but you'd better drink this now.'

'I'm not paralytic,' she snapped. 'I've only had two glasses of wine.'

'Which—thanks to the fact that you've put yourself on a starvation diet—seem to have gone straight to your head; and you won't be much use with a hangover tomorrow,' he said grimly. 'So just get fed and stop arguing.'

With that he walked out again, and Tessa drank some coffee, then cut herself a slice of what turned out to be game pie and with a roll and butter made a filling meal. As she ate she began to feel better. Still apprehensive, but healthier and less woozy.

She looked around while she ate her pie, and then walked around eating an apple. She wondered if Orme had bought any of the furniture in here himself, or if it was all old family heirlooms. If he had grown up with it and took it for granted, knowing it was beautiful and valuable but accepting it as a fact of life.

Nothing in Tessa's childhood home had been worth more than a few pounds. Before she left she had given it all away. She had loved both her parents, but there had been nothing she could take with her.

She picked up a delicate gold and enamel Fabergé egg, and was examining it when Orme came back. She replaced it, quickly but carefully, as though there was a notice somewhere, 'Please do not touch the exhibits.'

'Look at this.' He put a ring on a little table, beside the egg. 'It might fit you,' he said. 'She has small hands.'

'Who has?'

'My grandmother.'

Lady Ursula Jared. Tessa had heard of Lady Ursula. She must be nearing eighty, but she still photographed like a beauty, and she did not seem the sort of woman who would appreciate her jewellery being worn without permission. Unless she was here, and if she was what could Orme have told her?

'Does she know?' Tessa gasped.

'Not yet. She has a room here, but she lives in Gloucestershire.'

'And she leaves rings like this behind?'

'We have a wall safe, and this is hardly the Koh-i-noor.'

'It could have fooled me,' said Tessa.

'Try it on,' said Orme.

She stared as though the sparkling stone mesmerised her, holding her hands back and away as though this time she really must not touch. 'I—couldn't.'

He had her hand and before she could protest again he had slipped the ring on her finger. Tessa did not have particularly small hands, but her fingers were slim and this ring was an excellent fit. All the same, she would be scared to wear it. She asked, 'What would Lady Ursula say about me walking around flaunting her diamond?'

'Nothing. She can have it back in a few weeks.'

'But supposing I lost it?'

'Then I'd buy her another one if she wanted it.' He could, but that was not the point, and Tessa said with all the determination she could muster,

'I would rather not, and I'd rather not go on with this at all. It isn't necessary and it wouldn't work.'

'I think it necessary,' said Orme, and she knew that she really had told him everything. Not only in words, but in her voice and her eyes she had revealed what might happen to her if she met Paul again, and Orme was not going to let it happen.

'And it will work,' he said, 'we'll put it to the test right now. Annie and Spike's lights are on. We'll go up, show the ring to whoever's up there, and if they're not convinced I put it on your finger then I'll accept that we couldn't get away with it.'

'They'll think it's a joke.'

'Will they?' He came closer to her, putting a hand beneath her elbow, and as she stiffened instinctively he smiled. 'That would be giving the game away—flinching if I touched you.'

She could feel herself starting to colour. 'I wasn't flinching. I'm nervous, I guess.'

'Nervous of what?'

Of him. She had always been a little nervous of him, but never more than now. He was a power-house of a man, and in all the months she had worked for him she had never stood so close, with his hand on her. There had never been any confidences exchanged, certainly no secrets, but now he knew more about her than any of her friends did.

'Just nervous of making an even bigger fool of myself,' she admitted wryly, and his eyes glinted with amusement.

'Do you feel up to walking in on them with my arm around you?' he asked her gravely. 'Because if you don't they're going to think this is a strange affair.'

That made her smile too, and he said, 'You're too tidy.'

'What?'

He stood back, arms folded. 'Much too neat to have just weathered a passionate interlude. I'm all for the gentle touch, but that would have been ridiculous.'

She was laughing now, and so was he. 'This is crazy,' she said.

It was crazy to ask Spike and Annie to believe that Orme had been making love to her. Embarrassment was in her laughter too, and she ran her fingers through her hair, making much of the nonsense of transforming herself into a girl to whom something quite astonishing has happened.

'How's that?' she asked.

'Much better.' He sounded like he did at work when the action was going as he directed, but now there was that gleam of humour in his eyes. 'They'll expect you to have put your lipstick back on,' he said, 'but you look much more abandoned now.'

'Is that what we're after, the abandoned look?' She went across to the mirror to inspect herself. All she had done was mess up her hair. She should have looked as she often did, but the mirror had its own witchery and she saw a girl whose face was not quite the face she knew, whose eyes and hair were shadowy.

Deep in the warm glow of the mirror was the room in all its timeless elegance, and the man. She leaned forward, searching Orme's reflected face as though the mirror image would show her more than flesh and blood. But it didn't. Both faces had the same hard lines. Even the mirror couldn't soften his kind of toughness.

'Whatever you're looking for,' he said, 'you'll see it better facing the room.'

She turned back to face him. 'It's different from most mirrors, isn't it?' She gave it another sidewards glance. 'Last time I came here, for the party, I had to keep looking into it. It made everyone seem nicer somehow, gentler and prettier.'

'Old mirrors are kindly,' he said. 'What were you looking at?'

'You,' she blurted.

39

'And did I look gentler and prettier?'

She smiled at that. 'It doesn't seem to work so well for you.'

'No? Well, that would be asking rather a lot of it. Now shall we go and break the news to Spike and Annie?'

If he hadn't taken her arm she would have hung back, and gone on hesitating and arguing. But he guided her unceremoniously out of the room, and along the thickly carpeted corridor to the second flight of the back stairs.

The television was on. Words and music floated down from one of the closed doors above, and about half way up the stairs Tessa began to drag back. 'Please, I don't think I can——'

'You don't need to do a thing,' said Orme. 'Leave it to me.'

'They won't believe you. They'll die laughing.'

This staircase was much narrower than the main one. It wasn't easy to fit both of them on one step, and Orme still held her arm. Now he glowered down at her and she had her chin almost digging into his chest.

'You are not Alice through the looking glass in spite of your affinity for old mirrors,' he said with heavy sarcasm. 'And I would prefer not to lose a promising member of my team because she happens to be hooked on an illusion.'

'What's this if it isn't an illusion?' she gasped, and wriggled her ring finger.

'A protection, was how I think you described it. If you wear my ring it will keep golden boy away. It's up to you. But whatever you decide don't break your heart in my time.'

If she had any spirit in her surely she was proof against Paul Mellor. And she had spirit, and she was almost certain she could stay aloof even when she was back in the old surroundings. She was almost sure, but not quite certain she could manage without help.

She said, in a tight little voice that tried to be light, 'Once is enough for heartbreaking. Love is really very overrated!

'Appallingly so.' The deep voice rumbled in the deep chest beneath her ear, and she looked up in horror.

'Good grief, I've put lipstick all over your shirt!'

There were distinct smudges of coral fire on the cream silk shirt when he looked down at it. 'That's a nice touch,' he said. 'That should clinch the matter.'

'I know how to get it off,' she said quickly. 'Carbon tetrachloride, and then wash it.'

'You don't say,' he drawled, in mock appreciation of her know-how, smiling as he asked, 'Do you often get lipstick on and off shirts?'

'Jessie in the canteen told me,' she told him. 'I had some on a scarf I was wearing.' She grinned. 'My own lipstick on my own scarf. It works, but I haven't tried it out on a man's shirt before.'

Orme laughed, and at that moment Annie opened the door and looked down the stairs at them. She was in her late twenties, small and wiry like her husband, but pretty, and no one could say that of Spike. She had smooth dark hair, cut very short, and she was wearing a floppy blue sweater, blue jeans, and pink fluffy mules.

'Hello,' she said happily, and then, 'Hel*lo*,' on a different inflection, because Tessa did seem to be in Orme's arms. And then, as she realised she might have been tactless, she began to chatter. 'Come up.

41

Come in. How nice! Spike, it's Orme—and Bones. Isn't that super?'

'Super,' Spike mimicked her from inside the room, wondering what was putting the shrillness into her welcome. He had been watching television, but he was on his feet when they walked in.

This flat was entirely modern. It looked like the set of a TV commercial, except that it was untidy, lived-in and cosy, and Tessa always liked coming here. There were newspapers on the floor and a cushion on the rug in front of the fire—where Annie had been sitting before she'd heard someone on the stairs and gone to the door.

'Everything all right?' Spike asked. Seeing Orme and Tessa together he presumed it had to be a work problem, and he was looking worried.

'Very much so,' said Orme. He took Tessa's hand and held it towards them, and the ring flashed and they were both struck dumb. On the television screen people went on talking, and behind their talk the music played, but so far as the humans went there was complete silence.

Then Spike and Annie spoke together. 'You don't mean——' Spike got out, and gulped and left it.

'Bones and you?' squeaked Annie.

Tessa had known it would be like this and she tried to speak, but Orme said, 'That's right,' and this time Spike said,

'Well, I'm——' before he was at a loss for words again.

'Oh . . .' said Annie, as though she couldn't quite get her breath, and they were both smiling, laughing. They were surprised, astounded, but unbelievably they were not disbelieving.

Annie flew at Tessa, flinging both arms around her and kissing her heartily. She didn't kiss Orme, but she did squeeze his arm crying, 'But how lovely, how splendid. This is fantastic!'

That it is, thought Tessa. 'We had no idea, had we?' Annie gave her Spike a darting suspicious look, wondering if he had been holding out on her, and he disclaimed that with a wide grin.

'Not a clue, so help me.'

'It was rather sudden,' said Orme gravely.

'Very sudden,' said Tessa, getting in her first word.

She couldn't believe they were taking it this easily. This very afternoon Orme had been yelling at her for putting that report in her desk, instead of on his; and tomorrow it was quite likely he would be calling her everything under the sun for some other slip-up. And yet they believed he might have asked her to marry him. In spite of Miss Vella. In spite of all the signs he had of being a born bachelor. Who was it who said that the more whopping the lie the likelier it was of being swallowed?

'We must have a drink.' Spike was heading for the sideboard and Tessa said hastily,

'Not me, thanks, I've had enough. It's been——' It wasn't easy to sum up what it had been. 'Quite an evening,' she finished lamely, and saw Annie's dancing eyes and knew with a sinking feeling that she would have to invent that passionate interlude between herself and Orme, because Annie expected to be told about at least some of it.

Orme put an arm around her and she didn't flinch. She even managed to smile up at him, and if she flushed that was all right. 'We only looked in to tell you the news,' he said. 'You're the first we've told.'

They were flattered at that, and Orme and Tessa left them, still reeling but convinced that the ring

43

on her finger was a genuine announcement of intent to marry.

Back in the drawing room Orme grinned. 'What did I tell you? Unqualified success. Annie will be on the phone now to Freddie's wife, asking her if she had any idea what was going on under their husbands' noses.'

'That would be worth hearing,' Tessa said drily. 'They'll wonder how I managed it.'

'They're more likely to wonder how long you'll put up with me.' His deep voice was amused. 'Not an easy man to live with,' he intoned, and that was what people might say, and they might be right.

Tessa laughed. 'Well, I don't have to worry about that.'

'No.' He checked his watch. 'Do you want any more coffee?'

'No, thank you.'

'Then I'll take you home, and you'd better get a good night's sleep because I'll be round at eight in the morning in my other role.'

But he was only playing one role—that of her employer. All this was insurance against inefficiency. There would be no time out for heartbreak in his team or on his time.

'Thank you,' she said, quietly and sincerely.

'My pleasure.' He made her a half bow. 'In, of course, the most platonic sense of the word.'

'Of course,' and she was smiling again, although she wrinkled her nose when she said, 'But I'm still not happy about this ring.'

He made a dismissive gesture, sweeping her objections away. 'Consider it a piece of office equipment I've issued to you.'

'That's going to stretch the imagination.' You could hypnotise yourself with a ring like this. When

44

she moved her hand backwards and forwards it was like following a swinging star.

Orme had picked up her coat, and he held it while she slipped her arms into the sleeves. Then he held the door open for her, and they came out of the house again, into a night that was growing colder.

Tessa wondered if Annie might be watching from one of the two top windows and she glanced up, but the curtains were drawn, and anyway Annie was probably still on the phone. Or asking Spike yet again if he hadn't had any idea at all that Orme was likely to be asking Tessa to marry him.

As the car drew away from the pavement Orme began to talk about the first day's filming. That was featuring the old mine as it was now, and while they discussed shots Tessa saw each again in her mind's eye, the coalmine and the hills around.

It was five years since she had walked the hills, but she seemed to have total recall for even the shape of the trees, the cloud formations, how the gorse grew, during those five months that had spanned summer into winter. She could remember the clothes she wore. A blue dress and a dell in a little wood called Slade's Spinney, where the moss was soft as down, and she had sat with Paul, loving everything he said. He had fanned her with a giant fern to keep the midges at bay, and said she was a wood nymph.

She had been barefoot, she had pretty feet, and the moss was soft. It had been a good summer and her legs and feet were golden brown.

She went on answering Orme's questions, discussing their schedule with him, remembering the spinney, Paul's face, and the feel of the moss under her toes.

There was a little silence, a minute or two, but

45

she didn't realise Orme was going to change the subject and that they had finished talking work, until he asked, 'What's Paul's surname?'

'Er—Mellor, Paul Mellor.' It sounded as though she had half forgotten.

'What does he do?' Orme inquired casually.

'He's a lawyer, in his father's firm. Well, he was, I suppose he still is.'

'Do you get news of him? Do you keep in touch with anyone from there?'

'Not really. I know he married. Someone wrote and told me that three years ago.'

For over a week she had cried herself to sleep each night, and as she had been sharing a flat with two other girls it had meant covering her head with the bedclothes and weeping silently. One of the reasons why she had gone around with a splitting headache, and ended up being bullied by her flatmates into taking copious doses of tonic because they had decided she was run down.

She had known Paul would marry. She had even been told who he would marry. It was just that he still had this power to hurt her, or revive the memory of pain.

Now Orme said drily, 'If he has a wife she may have something to say about him fanning old flames. You probably won't need protection.'

'I hope I don't. But I had this Christmas card.' It was the middle of February now. 'I still send some Christmas cards there and I still get some. Not to Paul or his family, of course, but to some of the folk I used to know.'

Her voice sounded loud in the closed-in cabin of the car although she was speaking softly. Orme's eyes were on the road ahead, lit by the broad white ray of their headlamps. But he was waiting for her to go on and she licked her lips with the tip of her tongue. Her lips were dry. Her mouth was dry.

She coughed, clearing her throat. 'This one card,' she said, 'said, "We don't see Paul and Stella together these days. There's been a split there." '

'Were you glad about that?'

She wished he would stop probing. It was like using a scalpel on a wound. But she answered honestly because she had already told him so much, and because he would know if she didn't.

Something was cutting the palm of her hand. The ring had turned a little, so that as she sat with clenched hands the stone pressed into her flesh. She turned it back and held it between thumb and fingers. It was something to grip.

'Yes,' she admitted, 'for a moment I was glad. Then I realised that it had nothing to do with me, and if I went back there I could lose all I'd made of myself since I left the place. I could lose everything.'

That sounded melodramatic, but how did she know that she wouldn't go to pieces if she met Paul again?

'If that marriage is breaking up,' she said fervently, 'I want no part in the split.'

'That seems all I need to know,' said Orme.

Tessa was glad about that. She looked out at the familiar roads—they were getting near her home—and hoped they would arrive before he could think of any more questions to ask her.

When the car stopped she opened her own door. Orme wasn't seeing her up, why should he? 'Eight o'clock sharp,' he said.

'Of course.' When had she ever kept him waiting? She watched the car go, the ring feeling odd, heavy on her finger. It was freezing cold, and she dug her hands deep into her pockets as she turned towards her own flatlet block.

She wasn't surprised to see Mrs Prestcott's head come round Mrs Prestcott's door. 'You're back early.' Mrs Prestcott sounded disappointed, and you had to give her credit for that. She was a gossip and a nosey-parker, but she wasn't malicious. She preferred nice things to happen to people.

'We're starting early tomorrow,' Tessa explained as she began to hurry up the stairs.

'Ah!' said Mrs Prestcott, as though that was reassuring, raising her voice to keep up with the distance Tessa was rapidly putting between them. 'That was the man you work for, wasn't it? I've seen him before, haven't I? He's not the sort you'd forget in a hurry, is he?'

'Not in a hurry,' said Tessa from the top of the stairs. And that, she thought, could rate as one of the understatements of all time.

CHAPTER THREE

NEXT morning Tessa remembered, the moment she woke. First that this was the day she was returning to Blackstone, and then that Orme knew about Paul and that she would be under Orme's protection. Relief flooded her and she put on the ring like a good luck charm, something to ward off the evil eye.

At five minutes to eight the doorbell rang. It was Orme, and that was unusual. He was never late but rarely early, and she looked at her own watch, again very conscious of the ring on her finger. 'Sorry,' she said, 'I was just on my way down.'

'I thought you might be, so I came up. If we'd said our good mornings in front of Spike and Annie I'd have had to kiss you and that might have embarrassed you.'

'Of course it wouldn't,' she said, but it would have done.

He walked in and picked up her case. He was still wearing the camelhair overcoat, and a grey suit. The shirt was grey silk today and Tessa wondered if his housekeeper knew how to get the lipstick off the cream shirt. 'I'll bet she does, with all the experience she must have had,' she thought, and shifted her gaze quickly as though he might be reading her thoughts.

'Well, get your coat on,' he said.

She shrugged into it hastily. As she closed her flat door he said, 'Take my arm.'

'What?'

'For God's sake girl, we got engaged last night!'

'Oh, yes!' Annie would be waiting eagerly for her first sight of the happy couple together, and if Tessa trailed down, her usual two paces behind Orme, it would look like the start of a cool relationship. All the same, hanging on to Orme did not come naturally.

'I feel such a fool,' she muttered.

'You are a fool, Bones,' he told her genially. 'That's what this is all about,' and as she bit her lip he said, 'Don't worry about it. Foolishness is inherent in the human situation.'

'You mean there are a lot of us about?'

'Exactly. Join the club.'

'You too? I don't believe it.'

'That I'm a fool at times?'

This bantering was what she needed, and she said, 'I was thinking more of you being part of the human situation.'

'You're not suggesting I'm inhuman?'

'It has been suggested.' It had, by those who found him domineering and didn't know him very well. He *was* domineering when the need arose, but after last night most of Tessa's antagonism against him had been disarmed.

He was on her side, and she was grateful to him. As they came out of the flats he said, 'Is that a challenge? Do you want proof that I'm human?' and she laughed, feeling herself colouring, so that Annie was delighted, thinking that Bones had never looked prettier or happier.

Tessa was thinking that she had never blushed so much for years as she had in the last twelve hours. She had thought that was a childish habit she had outgrown. She could only hope that she had outgrown her childish habits, that mindless adoration of Paul Mellor most of all.

Usually Tessa sat in the back with Annie, but this

morning Spike was beside his wife, and Tessa was expected to take the front seat with Orme. Usually Tessa enjoyed the girls' gossip she and Annie kept up quietly in the back seat, but this morning she wasn't eager for that and she took the front passenger seat meekly.

Apart from the positioning of passengers nothing else on the journey showed any change of status. Orme was Orme, and Tessa was Bones, part of his team on her way to do a job of work.

The talk was mostly about work, and the car took the motorway at the top legal speed, going smoothly, without effort, with plenty of power held in check. His car was like him, Tessa thought. No matter how hard Orme Jared was working, or how fast he was moving, you always knew that there was still a reserve of strength.

She had often felt that the job stretched her to her limits, but Orme had said last night she was only beginning so perhaps she had more strength than she knew. She might need it. Sitting here, smiling and talking, her thoughts were racing ahead to their destination, and the nearer they came the quieter she became.

She couldn't help it. She tried hard to sound natural, but then she realised that she was starting to talk faster and shriller and silence was safer. She was in familiar surroundings now, within a few miles of Blackstone, noticing changes: rows of little houses replaced by faceless giant blocks, chapels and cinemas turned into warehouses or bingo halls or just standing derelict.

'You used to live round here, then?' said Annie.

'Yes.' Tessa laughed ruefully. 'The built-up areas were always fairly grim, but it used to be prettier than this.'

'Maybe the weather's got something to do with

it,' suggested Spike. It was a cold iron-grey day that would make anywhere look dreary, and the beauty of the area had always been the moorlands. They were dotted with coalmines, but there were rolling acres between that were wild and splendid.

Tessa looked through the car window and shivered. 'It looks so cold,' she said. Not much of a welcome home. But of course it wasn't her home.

Blackstone was a busy little town. They came into it in a stream of traffic, and reaching the roundabout that had once been an open square Orme asked, 'Which way?'

'Straight across.' She looked up the hill, rising to the right, with the church on the far skyline, and wondered if the little row of cottages where she was born still stood. The supermarket, in whose office she had worked, was flourishing and had taken over what used to be a baby-wear shop next door.

'Right up this road towards the hills,' said Tessa as Orme took the turning off the roundabout.

The road was crossed by others. Its name changed, the buildings along it changed, until it was a fine road from which the houses stood well back in cared-for gardens behind tall trees. Some houses were new, some old, but each was individual, architect designed.

'There are some smashing houses here,' Annie piped up.

'This is the exclusive end of town,' Tessa said gaily. 'If your address is Greenheath Avenue you've made it in Blackstone.' She sat, looking ahead, telling Orme, 'When you come to the hills, at the end of this road, you turn to the right, and about five minutes down that road is the Stag's Head.'

She had meant to keep looking ahead, as though there was no house in Greenheath Avenue that meant more to her than the rest, but as they passed the house where Paul had lived her head jerked round.

It was a reflex action, as irresistible as though somebody tugged her by the hair.

The big white house stood in the smooth green lawns that her father had tended, and it was bigger than she remembered. Another wing had been added. She remembered Paul talking about how the house could be enlarged, although it had always seemed vast to Tessa.

The new wing had probably been built for Paul and Stella, and she turned in her seat, straining to catch every possible detail. She didn't really want to see it, but she couldn't tear her eyes away.

'The Mellor residence?' murmured Orme pleasantly.

He knew too much. He saw too much. 'Why, yes,' she said, as though it couldn't matter less.

'Friends of yours?' asked Spike.

'My father was a gardener there, after the pit closed.' That was something she hadn't told Orme before. Orme knew that her father had been a collier and then a gardener, but he didn't know he had worked for Paul's father, and that Tessa had often run all the way up here, in her lunch hour, with any excuse she could think of to see her father, really on the offchance of seeing Paul.

She rarely did, and in those days Paul never saw her, even if he smiled and said hello; but walking through his gardens was worth going without her lunch.

What a little fool I was, she thought. What a long time ago that was. But she could still remember the breathless waiting, and the way the sun always seemed to shine when Paul spoke to her, even if the sky was overcast.

She said quickly, 'You'll like the Stag's Head. It

was an old hunting lodge in the days when all around here was called the Bishop's Chase. It's an interesting old place.' She began to tell them about its history, gabbling on.

The Stag's Head had been an inn for a long time, and in the summer it was popular with trippers. But at this time of year, when most of its trade was local in the bar in the evening, Tessa had had no difficulty getting rooms for six and the exclusive use of the small dining room as living quarters and office.

Six visitors' beds were all they had, and the landlord and his wife considered themselves lucky to be fully booked for three weeks in February. They were a Mr and Mrs Mann, newcomers since Tessa left.

She had been in here with Paul, it was his local, but it was also the only residential hotel in Blackstone, so she hadn't had much choice. And as it was on the hills, and so was the old coalmine, it was ideally situated.

All the same, she was glad that Mr and Mrs Mann wouldn't remember her. She didn't need reminding of her visits there with Paul.

The car park was behind a low wall, and from it you walked into the inn, a weathered redstone building, with a good 'period' atmosphere. The ceilings were low beamed, the woodwork was dark and polished, and there was always a log fire—genuine in winter, mock in summer—in the big fireplace in the main bar.

The TV van was among the few cars in the car park. Freddie and Jim had arrived, and Orme parked his car as near the entrance to the inn as possible. While Orme and Spike collected the luggage from the boot Annie grabbed Tessa's arm, holding her back, letting the men go on ahead.

54

She hissed, 'Bones, I've got such a bone to pick with you! You never told me a word. What about Derek?'

Tessa had taken Derek to dinner at Spike's and Annie's only last week. 'I—well——' she began helplessly.

'Not that I ever thought that was serious,' Annie whispered, 'but I never thought *Orme*.' Her eyes followed Orme's tall figure, walking in through the door, and she raised her voice a little now that he was out of sight, to ask, 'How did it happen?'

'Honestly,' said Tessa, 'I'm not too sure.'

Annie giggled. 'You know what Spike said?'

'Do I want to know?' Tessa wondered, and Annie went on giggling.

'He said, "Orme won't let it make any difference to his language if Bones gets any of her facts wrong."'

'Spike's right,' said Tessa.

She felt rather mean, deceiving Annie like this, but she was committed now, and as soon as they left here Annie and everyone else would understand why this engagement had turned out to be one of the shortest on record. 'We both had second thoughts' should be enough explanation.

The door opened into the bar, once the entrance hall of the lodge, and as the girls stepped in Freddie and Jim were both congratulating Orme, who was taking it with an aplomb Tessa envied.

'As for you,' said Freddie to Tessa, 'Joy's got it in for you. She says you've been holding out on her.'

'I'm sorry,' said Tessa huskily.

'It's all right, love,' he gave her a brotherly hug. 'Don't look so stricken.'

She couldn't look at Orme, she could hardly look at any of them. She had to smile and take their teasing and their good wishes, feeling a hypocrite and an idiot, and wishing she could hide her face, or better still herself.

Those few minutes seemed to last a long time, and worse was to come when she was handed the key to her room. She was on the top floor, a single room of course, but so was Orme, in the room next door. On the first floor Spike and Annie had a double room, flanked by two singles, into which Freddie and Jim had delivered their own luggage.

They obviously considered this arrangement would please all parties, and Tessa went wordlessly up to the top floor, opened her case, hung her coat in the wardrobe, and was waiting at the door of her room five minutes later when Orme came along the corridor.

There were only two bedrooms up here and they had a connecting door. Plenty of privacy, except that privacy wasn't required. She said, 'Freddie or Jim would have been in here, wouldn't they?'

'More than likely,' said Orme.

'They think——' She bit her lip and tried to smile, and felt that beastly blush burning her face again.

'Again, more than likely.' He stopped as he reached her, frowning as though she was being tiresome. 'But they don't know the facts, do they? I assure you your nights will be as undisturbed up here as they would have been down there.'

'I *know*.' It was just the looks of the thing that embarrassed her, not because she considered herself likely to loose any sleep through Orme coming to her door. Such a thought was unthinkable.

'Then stop looking as though you expect to be ravished any minute,' he said curtly, and strode on, into his room, while Tessa was stammering in impotent fury.

'I was not doing anything of the sort!'

She went back into her room, closing the door and beginning to unpack in feverish haste, grabbing clothes out of her case and stacking them into the small chest of drawers. The glimpses she caught of herself in the dressing table mirror made her admit that Orme had a point. She looked wild-eyed, her cheeks were flaming, and it was a real effort to slow down her breathing.

She looked like a girl in a tizzy, and indeed she was, more embarrassed than she had believed possible. Pretending an engagement to a man who didn't exist would have been a simple fiction, but pretending that Orme was the man she was going to marry was rife with embarrassing implications. Not to him, of course, nor to her, because they knew the facts. But the rest of the team thought they were lovers, and she was beginning to wonder if she would ever be able to look at him again without blushing scarlet.

She hung a shiny black trench coat mac in the wardrobe, beside her 'fur' coat, and heard the bang of a drawer from the other side of the dividing door. Sounds came through. The floor was carpeted, but he could probably hear her moving about, as she might hear him if she listened.

She had better get downstairs, lunch time was coming up, and then they were going across the hills for their first sight of the pit. It would be work as usual this afternoon and she was eager to get started. Eager to get finished too, and away from here and this silly subterfuge.

Orme knocked on her corridor door and called, 'Ready?'

'Coming.' She hurried, as always, as all of them did; and he was standing outside the door, waiting for her. When he saw her he demanded, 'Now what is it?'

'Nothing.'

'You still look as though you've just done a five-mile run.'

The few minutes unpacking her case hadn't been long enough to get back her poise and she blurted, 'It's more embarrassing than I thought it would be, that's all. I didn't realise they'd be giving us——' she gulped, and gasped, 'the bridal suite.'

Orme burst out laughing and she supposed it was bound to amuse him. She supposed it was funny really when they both knew that his only designs on her were to keep her in the team. 'With a door and a bolt between,' he said. 'But if it worries you we can change your room.'

'They would think I was a ninny, wouldn't they?' she asked slowly.

'They would rather, and so should I.'

Her smile was still a little unsteady, but she felt herself beginning to calm, relax. 'I'm sorry,' she said. 'I don't know why I'm making such a fuss, but it has been a bit embarrassing.'

He didn't deny that, but he said encouragingly, 'The worst's over. They'll just accept it now, until you're away from here safe and sound and can call the whole thing off. Ready for lunch?'

'Yes.'

This time he didn't tell her to take his arm as they walked downstairs, and Tessa was glad he didn't. They came down, talking about the afternoon's schedule, and she wondered if she would have been so worked up if Jim, say, or Derek, or anyone else had agreed to play the part of her fiancé.

She knew that she wouldn't. Perhaps it was because Orme was her boss, not unapproachable but a long way from being one of the lads, that made this change of relationship so traumatic. However you looked at it, there was an intimacy between them now that hadn't been there before. It wasn't physical, of course, and never would be, never could be, but it had her nerves jangling when nothing but her mind should be involved. What had happened to her common sense? What on earth could it matter that they had been put in adjoining rooms?

The closer the better. Well, not quite, but he was her protection here and she was standing now where she had stood with Paul.

When she'd walked in from the car park she had been caught up in Freddie and Jim's congratulations and she hadn't had time to think about anything else. But now she came down the stairs into the big room and saw that it had hardly changed at all.

Even the horse-brasses were in the same order. Mr and Mrs Mann must have liked the place as it was, they hadn't altered anything except the cushion covers on the chairs and settles, which had been rust-coloured cord and were now dark brown linen.

Spike was ordering pre-lunch drinks at the bar and Tessa sat with a Campari and soda in front of her, remembering that was what Paul had bought her the first time he brought her here. It was bitter, she had said, she didn't like it. The bitterness was to follow, but she hadn't known that then. Now her palate was more sophisticated and she sat among her colleagues, a career girl with a great future.

She recognised the woman behind the counter who was giving her some inquiring looks, not quite certain where Tessa's face belonged. She was going to come over and ask questions before long, so Tessa got up and went across herself and said, 'Hello, Margaret, do you remember me?'

Margaret Baker, a well-preserved blonde in her forties, still looked puzzled. She had worked here for the past twenty years, but she couldn't quite place Tessa. 'I knew I knew you,' she said.

'Tessa Harris. It's a long time. Five years.' Margaret was smiling but still at sea, and Tessa was surprised how casually she managed to say, 'I used to come in here with Paul Mellor.'

'Of course you did.' That completed the picture and gave Tessa a background. Margaret remembered her now and welcomed her as an old customer. 'Well, it is nice to see you again, and how's life treating you?'

'It's treating me very well,' said Tessa.

'You're in the television, then?'

'Yes.'

'Married, are you?'

'Not quite.' But Margaret had seen the ring.

'Very nice,' she said.

Tessa looked back at the group she had just left, sitting on settle and chairs round a table in a corner. 'That one,' she said.

Orme wasn't talking. Freddie was talking, Orme was listening with the rest of them, but he was the one the eye caught first, looking across at the group. You looked across and you knew which man gave the orders.

'Very nice indeed,' said Margaret again, and Tessa's stock soared.

Margaret remembered her now, as the little girl who had been one of the Mellor set for a while and had then vanished. 'Tessa's gone to London,' she remembered being told. 'She's got a job there.' Margaret had wondered at the time how that would work out, but the girl of five years ago had done well, improving almost out of recognition. And the man she was marrying looked somebody—probably more important than any man in this small town.

Tessa could guess what Margaret was thinking. She stayed a few moments longer, asking about Margaret's family, then she went back to her seat, on the end of the settle by Orme's chair.

'Getting news of old friends?' he asked.

'Margaret's family. She's a grandmother now.'

If she had stayed any longer Margaret would have told her about the men and women who were Paul's friends, and about Paul. She hadn't wanted that. She was going to hear about him soon enough, she was probably going to see him, but she wanted to delay both as long as possible.

In the meantime any moment someone she knew might arrive. The half dozen other customers were strangers to her, but somebody from her past could easily saunter in. Paul might, although Mr Mellor would disapprove of 'pubbing' in the lunch hour. Mr Mellor had a high opinion of his position and his dignity.

Even at her most starry-eyed Tessa had known that she failed to reach his standards in any way, and that he strongly disapproved of her friendship with his son. So had Paul's mother, but for a while Tessa had believed that no one could stop Paul loving her.

She looked at the door every time there was movement near it. Each time it was a stranger, and sometimes she met Orme's eyes and smiled. He never turned towards the door, but she knew that was because he read her expression. If she had recognised anyone he would have turned, and he'd have known Paul by the description she had given him. 'Golden-haired . . . like a Greek god . . .'

Perhaps in five years the gold would have dim-

61

med, but she could imagine Paul now, walking through that door, standing by the big fireplace.

Orme leaned towards her, speaking softly against her ear. It looked like a murmured endearment, but what he did say was, 'Stop it!' and Tessa knew he was reading her thoughts, although she whispered very softly back,

'What are you talking about?'

When they were signalled that their lunch was ready she was glad to get away. Yet, at the same time, almost disappointed, as though in her heart she *had* been hoping to see Paul.

Lunch over, they took to the hills, well wrapped up against the cold. The man who was taking them to the Grey Lady pit had arrived during the meal, joined them and been introduced all round. He was a Coal Board official, a local man, interested to hear that Tessa's father had worked at the Grey Lady, but he had never met Arnold Harris, nor Tessa until today.

They wanted some shots of the mine. There was an hour or so of light left, and the gaunt hills under the grey skies seemed a suitable setting for the silent colliery.

It had changed, of course, since Tessa saw it last. The grasses and the heather had grown thicker between railway lines and split open the concrete roads. The buildings were all windowless, most of the superstructure had been dismantled, the rest was rusting away. It looked desolate, dead.

Tessa held her clipboard in gloved fingers, snuggling into the long woollen scarf she had wrapped around her head and shoulders, her breath freezing.

She worked, as she always did, with a single-minded intensity that kept out most outside distractions, and most of the cold. This, she told herself, was a job of work like any other.

When the filming finished the men, with their equipment, headed for warmth and shelter as fast as they could. No one noticed that Tessa had fallen back. Orme was talking to the Coal Board man, well ahead of her, with Spike and Freddie and Jim just behind him.

Annie kept out of the way while work was being done. There was a tacit understanding that she could come on most trips, but nobody got in the way of the workers. So there was no Annie around right now.

Tessa lingered, until the men were out of sight. They were walking quickly, it was bitingly cold, but she stood on the iron bridge that ran over the railway line, looking across the hills.

She knew the hills well. The only change here was the change of the seasons, and now they were in the grip of winter. Night was coming down fast, but she could find her way back blindfold, although the path she used to take back led to the church at the top of Church Hill and the third cottage in a row of eight cottages.

She walked very slowly down the steps of the bridge. The tracks were the same. Miners no longer came to the pit, but the hills were still crossed by the old familiar paths, and she thought—the last time I walked this way I was walking to meet Paul.

It had been winter then, as cold as now, and Paul should have met her. But he hadn't. She had reached his house, and he had apologised that something had turned up to delay him, and she should have realised that she had become a nuisance, that he was tired of her.

At the beginning they had met about here, and when they saw each other they had hurried, and she had run into his arms. She stood still again, closing her eyes, surrendering to memories; and heard Orme calling her name.

That jarred her back. He was coming back through the dusk, looking immense in the distorting light. 'Are you all right?' he asked.

'Yes, of course.'

'You haven't turned your ankle, or some such nonsense?'

It was uneven underfoot, but she couldn't imagine why he thought she might have crippled herself. 'Of course I haven't,' she said, and he said irascibly,

'Then why are you standing around as though you've been immobilised?'

'Why not? We've finished work, haven't we?' If she wanted to walk slowly back, alone, to the Stag's Head, why shouldn't she?

'Normally,' said Orme, 'you could bivouac out here all night if you liked. But as you're supposed to be my fiancée of twenty-four hours it would have been considered remiss if I hadn't returned to collect you.'

'Oh! Sorry! I was admiring the view.' The view was diminishing as the dusk deepened. 'It used to be my back garden,' she said. 'I was born in a cottage over there.'

'A beautiful garden,' said Orme, 'but if you stay admiring it much longer you're going to freeze.'

Her scarf had fallen off her head, and he lifted the top fold to make a cosy head covering again, wrapping a couple of loops snug and warm around her neck. He did it quickly and deftly, but Tessa was so surprised that she stood blinking. 'You're halfway to a block of ice right now.' His fingers brushed lightly against her cheek. 'And I warn you, if you go down with the 'flu I will make your life hell.'

'I won't. I promise.' Her voice sounded breathy as she kept up with his stride. She had been cold, but walking fast was warming her, and for some reason her skin was tingling. Especially her cheek, where he had just touched her, as though there was a particularly sensitive nerve there.

She felt the touch still, and wondered if it was recalling Paul's arms around her that had quickened her senses.

Walking back with Orme left her no chance to think of Paul. Orme was asking now about the countryside, and she described the beauty spots and the places of interest until she felt like a walking guide book. Not that there'd be much chance of sightseeing. While they were here they would be working all hours.

'You've never been homesick?' he asked her, and she was getting a little nostalgic about the places she was describing.

'Sometimes.' She said quietly, 'But you know why I daren't come back.'

He knew, this big man walking beside her as night came down on the hills. 'For fear of ghosts?' he said. 'Is this one of the paths where ghosts walk?'

'What?'

'If your home was over there this would be the quickest way to the Mellor house,' he said in his slow deep voice, and she wished he was less quick on deduction.

'I was never exactly welcomed in the Mellor house,' she explained.

'Why not?'

Because Paul's parents had wanted him to marry Stella Spencer. They had thought that Stella was suitable wife material, but for all that it seemed the marriage was not wearing well.

'Because,' said Tessa, 'my father had been their

jobbing gardener, and I worked in a supermarket.' She summed it up. 'Because Mr and Mrs Mellor were grade A snobs,' and when Orme chuckled she smiled wryly. 'Oh, it's funny enough now, but it wasn't then.'

Yellow lights were glowing in the windows of the Stag's Head on the skyline, and the moon was out, a cool silver disc in a dark pewter sky.

Still smiling, Orme asked her, 'What did they look like, this couple who produced a Greek god?'

'Handsome,' she said promptly. 'Tallish and ever so well groomed, with never a hair out of place.' Laughing at them took away the sting of Mrs Mellor's cutting remarks and Mr Mellor's bruising brusqueness.

The path was narrow and the turf was rough, but Tessa and Orme walked side by side, watching their step. 'I suppose they might have had golden hair once,' she mused. 'But I can only remember him with silver grey and her with a blue rinse.'

'Handsome,' said Orme, and as she wobbled slightly, stepping on a stone, 'Watch it!'

'You watch it,' she retorted gaily. 'You could come down heavier than me.'

'That is something to consider,' he said.

The lights of the inn looked welcoming, and so did the room when they pushed open the big door and stepped inside. The bar was not open to the public yet, but Spike and Annie and Jim sat round the log fire, chatting with the landlord, a cheerful man with a florid complexion and a booming laugh.

He was booming now and the scene was full of bonhomie, but Tessa needed to get out of her coat and scarf and boots. She wanted to change, and she needed a little time to herself before she joined the crowd for the evening.

She said hello to Annie and crossed to the stairs, as Orme hung his coat on a coat rack and took a seat by the fire.

Tessa went upstairs alone. There was no one about on the top floor, and she hurried in and out of the bathroom. They were lucky, only two of them sharing this bathroom. Four had to share on the floor below.

Then she took her time choosing a change of clothing. She had worn navy trousers, and a couple of thick sweaters under her trench coat, during the day; but now she decided on a pink silk shirt, and a pink skirt, purple-flecked.

The colours were soft and flattering, and she sat at the dressing table carefully applying mascara, taking especial care with her appearance because tonight she was almost certain to be meeting somebody who remembered Tessa Harris.

Margaret Baker could have passed on the news since lunch time, and anyhow the TV team would be an attraction in themselves. Folk would be dropping in to have a look at Jim's well-known face; and to anyone who knew anything about the world of the small film Orme Jared was a famous name.

The men and women who had made up Paul's circle had never really been Tessa's friends, but she was human enough to want to surprise them when they turned up to take another look at little Tessa Harris after all these years.

She heard Orme in the next room and went on brushing her hair, because she was tense and this was relaxing. She wanted to look as good as she possibly could for the ordeal ahead. She glossed her lips and sprayed perfume on her pulse points, and when Orme rapped on her door she was just about ready.

'Coming!' she called.

'Yes,' he said as she stepped into the corridor, 'you'll do.'

'Do for what?'

An eyebrow lifted. 'For whatever you had in mind.'

'Just dinner.' She shrugged . 'And sitting around.'

'And watching the door?'

She walked a little ahead of him. 'Somebody I know is bound to come in sooner or later. It's rather like waiting for a time fuse to go off.'

'Or a lover to arrive?' Orme suggested, and at the top of the stairs she stopped with a little nervous gesture of protest.

'Why do you say that? You know that's not true.'

'Do I?' He had deep set eyes and heavy lids. Usually it would have been hard to tell the colour of his eyes, but now he looked straight at her and his eyes were grey as steel, and as hard. 'Do you?' he said.

Tessa would have told him there was no way she would have taken all this trouble with her appearance just because of Paul. If Paul should turn up she didn't want him to find her attractive. Of course she had tried to look good, but not for a lover. Orme knew that she didn't want to start anything going with Paul again, that it was the last thing she wanted. That was why she was wearing his ring.

She would have said all that if Orme hadn't walked past her, down the stairs. She needed a moment or two before she could follow, to get back her breath because she had another worry now. That Orme was beginning to lose patience just when she was needing his support.

The bar was filling, but Tessa didn't look at the newcomers. She went straight across to where Orme was standing by the fire, talking to Annie, and touched his arm. She could hardly carry on the conversation they had just been having, but she hoped he would understand that she was saying—I want the future you promised me, I don't want to get dragged back into my past.

She smiled as he turned, and he put an arm around her. He went on with what he was saying to Annie, and held Tessa, and she felt safe and comforted. So much so that she leaned against him lightly, her head on his shoulder, as though his strength could flow into her.

Then she looked around. She didn't care now who saw her. Linked with Orme she could face Paul, or any of them.

There was a familiar face. A girl perched on one of the bar stools was Jackie Goodman, who lived in Greenheath Avenue and whose father was a local bank manager. Well, that was where she had lived and her father's occupation five years ago, but the man with her was Roger Fielding and it was more than likely that she was Jackie Fielding by now.

Margaret, behind the bar, had been talking to them, and as Tessa looked across Jackie waved, and slid off her stool. Jackie and Roger were Paul's friends, but they had been amiable enough to Tessa and when Jackie said, 'Hello, stranger,' she sounded pleased to be renewing the acquaintance.

This was a different Tessa Harris, and young Mrs Fielding was impressed—by Tessa's looks, by the success she had obviously made of her career, and most of all by the man who stood beside her.

There were introductions. Tessa didn't find it too easy to say 'My fiancé,' but the words came out, and when Orme spoke to her Jackie went into quite a flutter. Women often did, with Orme around. Tessa had seen it happen before. And then Roger came over and met the team, who all believed that Tessa was enjoying herself, meeting old friends.

Jackie gave her the local gossip. You remember so-and-so and so-and-so, and then, inevitably, 'You heard about Paul and Stella?'

'I had a Christmas card from Mandy,' Tessa said lightly. 'She said something.'

'Stella's gone back to Mum. He's still at home— they had another wing built on.' Jackie grimaced. 'Stella comes in here sometimes, so Paul keeps away.'

'Oh,' said Tessa. 'Now tell me, where are you living?' And she listened, with every sign of interest, to Jackie's description of her and Roger's bungalow.

Work was the subject over the evening meal; and for half an hour or so afterwards the team stayed in their private room, holding a conference on tomorrow's shooting schedule.

Interviews had been set up, and while the format of these was being discussed Annie curled in an armchair, reading her magazine. When Orme said, 'That's it, then,' closing the folder that was open on the table in front of him, the rest of the evening was theirs; and the most comfortable way to pass it was obviously in the lounge-bar.

Spike and Annie, and Jim and Freddie, went off down the corridor. Tessa would have gone with them, but Orme had said, 'Bones, hold on a moment,' so she waited, her mind still busy with all they had been discussing.

'Get your coat on,' he ordered.

She was the research girl right now, and he was the director, and she thought they were off to check something out for tomorrow. Not that Orme usually helped her with her checking. 'Where are we going?' she asked.

'Out.'

You didn't argue when Orme gave an order. Tessa went upstairs and put on her trench coat and her long scarf. Orme was waiting at the bottom of the stairs, with his coat on, and he took her through the big brightly-lit room, from the sound of voices and laughter, into the car park.

It was cold outside, of course, and they walked quickly to the car. As soon as she was inside Tessa asked again, 'Where are we going?'

'Visiting.' He turned the ignition key, while she was frowning, trying to work that out.

'Who are we visiting?'

'The Mellors,' said Orme.

CHAPTER FOUR

'OH no!' gasped Tessa. It would take them about seven minutes to get to the Mellors' house. She wasn't prepared and she didn't think she could face it. She plucked at Orme's sleeve as he turned out of the car park, but he held the car on its course— there was a crossroads just ahead—and he was obviously in earnest.

'Please, *no!*' she pleaded.

'You're going to have no peace of mind until you've seen Paul Mellor again,' he said, and she cried shrilly,

'What makes you think I'll feel better after I've seen him?'

'No guarantee.' Of course there was no guarantee. It might be the end of her peace of mind for ever. 'But if this could be an explosive situation,' Orme continued, as though he was dealing with a problem in tomorrow's work plan, 'we should at least attempt to defuse it.'

Very sensible, except that she was quaking with panic. 'I don't want to see him!' she wailed.

'And I don't want you with half your mind on your work.' They were driving down Greenheath Avenue now. She couldn't stop him. He was taking her to the Mellors' door and she asked him wildly,

'What shall I say? "I've come to see Paul. Remember me, Paul, I'm the one who wrote the letters"?'

'Did you write a good letter?' His voice sounded the way she knew well, deep and amused.

She watched the houses and remembered who

had lived in them in this best end of town. 'I wrote a lot of letters,' she said, with bitter derision. 'Somebody told me they were all reading them in the end. They must have made hilarious reading.'

'Paul Mellor sounds a shade indiscreet,' said Orme. 'Particularly for a lawyer.'

'I was the indiscreet one.' The more she told herself that the less likely she was to repeat her mistakes. 'Any day I didn't see him I wrote to him. Imagine that!'

'Good practice for script-writing,' said Orme, as they turned into the drive of the Mellor residence.

'I don't want to go in here,' Tessa whimpered. 'I don't.'

'Are you proposing running for it?'

'Why don't you mind your own business?' As the car stopped she glared at him like someone cornered, as indeed she was, and he said crisply,

'You made it my business when you told me the story and accepted my help.'

'I didn't want this sort of help—shoving me into the lions' den.'

'The Mellors don't sound much like a pride of lions to me.' He got out, came round and opened her door. The old antagonism against him was stirring in her again. He *was* one of the most overbearing men alive, he *was* a juggernaut; but the idea of the Mellors as a pride of lions almost made her smile.

And she was more than likely to meet Paul again before she left Blackstone, and the best form of defence was supposed to be attack. And, unless she took to her heels, and a fine fool that would make her look, she had no choice but to walk up to that door with Orme, because the curtain of the lounge window was twitching, so their car had been heard, their arrival noted.

'Remind me to do you a good turn some time!' she hissed.

'I'll rely on it,' he said, and in spite of everything she laughed.

Orme rang the bell. She remembered the sound of it, just as she remembered the glimpse of the hall through the inset glass panel in the door. The door was mock old, the glass flawed to match so that the scene behind looked like something in a distorting mirror. Not a lovely old mirror, like the one in Orme's home, more like a nightmare image.

She could see someone coming, and she was holding Orme's arm. Holding tight, because if she hadn't held on she just might have turned and run.

It was Mrs Mellor. Another sign of the changing times—the Mellors had always had a resident maid who opened the front door. But, with the light behind her, Mrs Mellor showed no great change.

She was a tall woman, wearing a classic suit, blazer jacket and slim straight skirt in a harebell jersey silk. Her silver hair was impeccably waved, she hadn't even changed her hairstyle. She had changed so little that Tessa expected instant recognition, and one of those acid little comments that Mrs Mellor had gone in for while Paul was dating Tessa. Gibes about Tessa's clothes, her voice, her taste in anything.

But Mrs Mellor only said, 'Yes?' and Tessa stepped forward so that the hall light showed her more clearly. She said,

'Good evening, Mrs Mellor, I don't suppose you remember me.'

Mrs Mellor peered, then said in wonderment, 'It isn't—Tessa Harris?'

'That's right,' said Tessa, sounding bright and

74

cheerful, and not sure whether she was putting on this show for Mrs Mellor or for Orme. At the back of her mind was a determination not to let Mrs Mellor get the better of her in front of Orme. 'I'm with a TV team,' she announced breezily. 'We're doing a documentary around the Grey Lady pit and staying at the Stag's Head.' She smiled a wide smile. 'So I'm taking the chance to say hello again to some old friends.'

'Oh!' Mrs Mellor was quite taken aback. 'Do come in,' she said, automatically rather than with any real welcome.

As Tessa stepped into the hall she didn't look around, she looked at Orme. The hall wasn't as spacious as she remembered. Five years ago it was the most magnificent house she had ever entered, but since then her horizons had widened. And Orme, with his height and presence, helped to cut it down to size.

'This is Orme Jared,' said Tessa. 'Orme, Mrs Mellor.'

Orme was very dignified and very courtly. He bowed over Mrs Mellor's hand, and gave the impression that he was delighted to meet her; and Mrs Mellor looked taken aback all over again, but this time her welcome was much warmer.

'Orme is our director,' Tessa explained.

'Ah!' Mrs Mellor wasn't surprised at that. She had expected no less.

'And my fiancé,' said Tessa demurely. It was easier to say this time. She enjoyed saying it, and she was toying with the idea of removing her glove and flashing her ring in Mrs Mellor's face when Mr Mellor walked into the hall.

There were a few more lines on his face, and on Mrs Mellor's now that Tessa saw her under direct lighting, but he was still as neatly turned out and he still looked pompous.

'George,' his wife cried, 'you'll never guess who this is!'

'No, my dear.' He was looking at Orme, he hadn't even noticed Tessa. He never noticed her in the old days if he could help it. He would look straight through her, walk round her, but that was a deliberate snub. This time he looked at Orme because everybody did, and Tessa could have burst out laughing.

Mrs Mellor had meant him to look at Tessa, who was the surprise guest, but she quite understood that Orme took precedence, and she proceeded with introductions. 'Mr Jared, my husband George. George, this is Mr Jared. He's a television director and——'

Mr Mellor advanced beaming, with an outstretched hand. 'Indeed I've heard of you, Mr Jared. Welcome to Blackstone, it's a very great pleasure to meet you. Now what can we do for you?'

Orme drew Tessa forward. 'I believe you and Tessa know each other.'

Mr Mellor blinked and Mrs Mellor said sweetly, 'It's Tessa, George, Tessa Harris.'

He still could hardly remember her. She had been a tiresome girl with a crush on Paul, over whom Paul had made a young fool of himself, but not for long. Once it was over it had been best forgotten, filed in the dusty drawers of his mind. Tessa said, 'The gardener's daughter. A long time ago,' and had the pleasure of seeing that sink in.

He recovered quickly—he wasn't a lawyer for nothing—and smiled quite paternally at her. 'Why, so it is. My dear young lady! Come along in. Come and let us hear all your news.'

The lounge door was open and he ushered them

through it as though they were VIPs. Orme was, of course, but there was irony in this for Tessa. Mr Mellor had never directed her towards the lounge before, he had always acted as though she should consider herself favoured if she got a foot into the kitchen.

Mrs Mellor was explaining, 'They're doing a programme about one of the coalmines.'

'So I heard,' said Mr Mellor, 'and is Tessa——'

'A working member of the team?' Orme continued smoothly. 'Very much so. She has a great future.'

Mrs Mellor, who was taking their coats, said with an arch smile, 'They're engaged to be married,' and Orme smiled and said,

'I was speaking professionally.' He took Tessa's hand, held it steadily and firmly and looked at her with steady eyes. 'But in every way,' he said, 'I hope her future will be happy and successful.'

Professionally he meant, and in any private life that didn't interfere with the job. No falling in love so that love came first. No losing her head as she had done with Paul. Orme was here to block out the memories, and he did. Most of them.

As soon as they were seated Mr Mellor offered drinks. 'No, thank you,' said Tessa, but Orme said yes, and Mr Mellor poured whisky for himself too; while Mrs Mellor insisted on going away and preparing coffee for Tessa with her own hands.

'We have a daily now,' she confided to Tessa. 'Getting staff is getting worse all the time, isn't it?'

'Mine's a very labour-saving flat,' said Tessa, and thought better of drawing Orme into that conversation. His housekeeper was undoubtedly a treasure, but she doubted if he would care to discuss her with Mrs Mellor.

Mrs Mellor returned with the coffee tray, and

drew up a small table for herself and Tessa. The silver coffee set, no less, and the Royal Doulton china, and Mrs Mellor inquiring, 'Cream and sugar?' in her most affable hostess manner.

Tessa had seen that in action, but not for her. Not from the first time Paul had brought her home. This room was much the same—the same well-matched furniture, the grey walls, the unblemished grey carpet, and the occasional pastel pale Chinese rug. Tasteful and dull, although once it had petrified her with its perfection.

She had once spilt a drink on that carpet, putting down a glass that Paul had given her, and jumping up nervously when his mother came into the room so that she kicked it over. She had been almost weeping from sheer shame in her clumsiness, and Mrs Mellor, tight-lipped and furious, had snapped that the carpet was ruined, that it would be impossible to remove the stain, ever.

There was no sign of a stain now. It would have been just there, under Orme's feet. Unless the carpet had been moved around, or this was a new one, a double of the old.

Tessa found her mind wandering back to that kind of silly incident while she drank her coffee and joined in the conversation.

Mr Mellor, at least, was interested in the TV film and Orme was giving Tessa such a build-up that they must have believed she was his right hand. None of it was untrue. She did do the research, and arrange interviews, and sometimes she helped to write the scripts. But everything Orme said exaggerated her importance so that Mr and Mrs Mellor were looking at her with ever-increasing surprise and respect, and she didn't know where to look.

Orme could charm anybody, his team all knew

that, and when he grinned across at Tessa she laughed with him. He had drawn the bitterness out of these two for her. She had always known they were snobs, but their contempt had once hurt her deeply. There was no contempt now. They were falling over themselves to be friendly.

Orme knew the cream of the legal profession—the cream of most professions, thought Tessa a shade cynically—and when the name of a topline QC came up so did Paul's. 'My son prepared a brief that Mr Lander accepted about a year ago,' said Mr Mellor, and Orme said, as though that reminded him,

'Your son? That would be Paul? We were hoping to meet him.'

He smiled at Tessa, as though Paul was on her list of old friends. No more than that, but someone she remembered with affection and would be happy for her fiancé to meet.

'But certainly.' Mr Mellor was enthusiastic, and Tessa wondered if he had forgotten that she had left this town because of Paul. If he remembered he had decided that the years between had wiped the pain away, and that now there was no emotion left.

He should be right. That should be the way it was. But all the time Tessa had been in Blackstone, let alone in this house, she had been waiting to hear Paul's voice or see him walk through the door. She wasn't indifferent. She was protected, but she was not immune, and it was no good telling herself that she was.

Mrs Mellor was on her feet, smiling, saying, 'Of course, Paul would never forgive us if we let you go without telling him,' but Tessa felt that Mrs Mellor was less willing than her husband to get Paul into this room.

Perhaps her memory of five years ago was clearer than her husband's. Perhaps it was because Tessa could hardly breathe herself, now that she was within minutes of seeing Paul again, that she thought Mrs Mellor's smile had become strained.

But Mrs Mellor might as well fetch Paul, because Orme meant to get that first meeting between Paul and Tessa over as soon as possible. If Paul had not been home tonight there would have been a future date arranged. Orme would have fixed it. There was an inexorable quality about Orme. He was both the irresistible force and the immovable object, even if that was a contradication in terms; and Tessa glared at him while Mr Mellor meandered on.

Mr Mellor had no idea that she was glaring. His attention was all with Orme, who smiled blandly at Tessa, and went on encouraging Mr Mellor's flow of legal anecdotes.

Mrs Mellor didn't return in a hurry. She was away for almost ten minutes and Tessa was beginning to hope that Paul might not be home after all. If he was she wondered if he was still using the wing that had been built on to this house for himself and his bride. Or if that was quiet and unlived-in and he was once more under his father's roof, back in the bedroom he had had as a bachelor.

Tessa had never seen that room, she had never seen any of the rooms upstairs. Long ago, after she and Paul had said goodnight, she would lie in her own little bed and imagine Paul sleeping, imagine what his room was like. In her dreams she was in his dreams.

There was no sound of footsteps, the hall was carpeted. The door opened and Mrs Mellor and Paul came in, and Tessa's heart leapt as it used to do when he galloped by on horseback, the most beautiful man in the world.

He was still a Greek god. Although what had she expected five years to do to a young man, leave him bald and wrinkled? Five years wasn't very long. In sunlight his hair would be gold. It was fair, light brown, his skin was smooth and his eyes were blue. He had regular chiselled features and a lovely straight nose, and as he walked across the room towards her the years slipped away.

'Tessa.' he said.

'Hello, Paul.'

They both smiled. She held out a hand to him and he took both hands. He said, 'They must have been five good years, the way you look.'

'They were.' Yes, they were. She had watched that no man hurt her again. She had found good friends, and work she enjoyed. 'And life's getting better all the time,' she said.

She felt, rather than saw, Orme stand up, then he was towering behind Paul, like a shadow falling over her. She said what she had to. 'This is Orme Jared, Orme—Paul Mellor.'

They shook hands and Paul said, 'You're a lucky man.'

His mother had told him, of course. He hadn't needed to see the ring on Tessa's finger, that suddenly felt as heavy as a fetter.

'I know it,' said Orme.

It was all very friendly, very comfortable. Paul sat down and asked for the news. He knew all about the TV team. He didn't say that anyone had told him Tessa was with them, but she sensed that that bit of gossip had reached him. Although it hadn't reached his parents until tonight.

This time Orme let Tessa speak for herself, and she answered Paul's questions about her work and the places it took her, while Orme and Mr Mellor went on talking together.

'You'll have heard that Stella and I broke up,' said Paul quietly.

'Yes, I had—I'm sorry,' said Tessa.

'That's life.' Paul smiled bravely and began to tell her about mutual friends. His friends. The people Jackie had told her about a couple of hours ago. From people to places, and he was talking about the changes around here in the last five years.

There was a roadhouse that was now under new management. Country walks that had been incorporated into new estates. Paul talked apparently casually, but everywhere he mentioned had a special meaning because he and Tessa had been there together. He must remember as clearly as she did. And no one else knew.

His mother was listening, joining in, but Mrs Mellor didn't know why the mention of Slade's Spinney made Tessa smile when Paul smiled at her.

Smiling she glanced across at Orme, and he looked back from heavy-lidded eyes. Instinctively she put a hand before her mouth, she didn't want him realising that she and Paul were playing a sort of game, and when Orme said, 'I think we should be going,' she jumped up nervously.

It reminded her of the time she had kicked over the wine glass. Paul had said, 'Don't fuss, Mother,' and afterwards he had comforted Tessa, 'Don't worry, forget it.'

Now it seemed that there were many things he hadn't forgotten. He had married his parents' choice, but he had remembered the gardener's daughter, who had spoken with what his mother had described as 'an appalling Black Country accent' in those days. But who had found she had a quick ear, and could pass for what Mrs Mellor would call a lady now in any company.

That might amuse the team, thought Tessa. She hadn't done her native accent in years.

They said goodnight all round. 'We must arrange something while you're here,' said Paul. 'We can get some friends in. Would you come?' He asked Orme, who said,

'Of course, we'd be delighted.'

Paul held Tessa's hand several seconds longer than necessary, coming out to the car with them and standing there as the car drove away.

'You described them well,' said Orme.

'Did I? They haven't changed much.'

'No. Well, how do you feel?'

They were out of the drive and into the avenue, and she would have preferred to sit quietly rather than undergo second degree. She said, 'All right.'

'No regression to adolescence?'

'I wasn't an adolescent.' Seventeen, eighteen when it ended. But she had adored Paul Mellor from childhood into teenage. 'Anyhow,' she said, 'he knows I'm supposed to be engaged. He won't——'

Orme chuckled. 'I wouldn't rely on that. He doesn't appear to be too observant.'

'*What?*' She turned to stare furiously at the dark figure beside her. 'Oh, I know he's not up to your giant intellect, but then who is?'

'He isn't up to my size either,' said Orme cheerfully. 'And if that really had been my ring you're wearing I'd have shaken hands with him when we said goodnight so that he wouldn't have forgotten again in a hurry.'

'What *do* you mean?' Her voice was shrill, but Orme's sounded as though he was smiling.

'That trip he was taking you down Memory Lane could have been chancing his luck.'

Idiotically Tessa felt guilty, as though she had been caught cheating. 'Memory Lane?' she stammered, and he reeled them off.

'The Goat at Edgebridge, Druid's Ring, Slade's Spinney, Five Springs.'

Everywhere that Paul had mentioned. Orme must have heard every word while he seemed deep in conversation with Mr Mellor. 'They were all supposed to mean something, of course,' he said, and why should she deny it?

'Yes,' she said. 'Silly things, but yes.'

'The language of lovers,' said Orme. 'Charming.'

She scowled, biting her lip. 'But not while I'm around,' he added. 'I find it hard to act like a bloody fool.'

If she really had been engaged to Orme it would have been disloyal to relive memories with Paul while Orme sat there, even though it had seemed a secret language at the time. Perhaps that made it worse, more like cheating.

She said, 'Sorry, I forgot the old saying, "There's nothing gets past Orme." So it's true you have eyes in the back of your head?'

'And ears,' he said. 'Why do you think I wear a toupée?'

'You *what*?'

Orme's hair was thick and springy, cut short but curling slightly. Here and there the dark brown was flecked with grey. Tessa had a crazy impulse to reach and touch, pretending to tug for a non-existent wig, laughing at the joke. But she didn't. Instead she latched her fingers together and was glad they were nearly at the Stag's Head.

The car park was far from full, but most cars were near the inn, and when Orme parked they were in the shadows. Tessa turned to open her door, but he

84

said, 'So Paul Mellor has memories too.'

'It seems so.'

'Does that surprise you?'

'I don't know.' Through the windscreen ahead were the moors, shining with frost in the moonlight. If she looked towards the inn there would be a warmer light, and people. She wished Orme would let her get into the inn. She said slowly, 'Yes, I think it did surprise me. Those places meant a great deal to me. The Goat—Paul used to take me to dinner there. I can remember what we ate, what we talked about. Well, what he talked about. Most of the time I just hung on his words.' She smiled wryly. 'I should have thought they would have been quite forgettable evenings for him.'

Perhaps they were. Perhaps he simply remembered he had eaten there with Tessa. 'We had a picnic once at Five Springs,' she went on. 'It was early autumn, but it was like a summer day. And Druids' Ring we walked round one Sunday afternoon. It started to rain and we had to run back to the car.' She laughed a little. 'You have to walk all the way round to get your wish, so maybe that's why mine didn't come true.' She grimaced. 'What rubbish I'm talking!'

'No,' said Orme. 'But remember it all. The end of the affair as well as the beginning.'

The end had been cold. There had been no one to turn to. She had been adrift in a shoreless sea, and now she stretched out a hand to touch Orme, just for the feel of human contact.

He moved slightly, wrapping her in his arms, so that she was held against him like a child being comforted. She huddled close, her cheek pressed against his chest, feeling the slow rise and fall of his breathing. His arms were strong around her. If she had known someone like Orme in those days she would have run to him.

In a way she had. She had run and she had met Orme and, although it was odd that he should be comforting her for a hurt of five years ago, he was doing just that. 'All right?' he asked after a moment or two.

'Yes.' He held her away, just a little, as though it was time she supported herself again, and she sat up, although she was reluctant to move. It had felt warm and pleasant with his arms around her. 'Thanks for everything,' she said.

'All in a good cause.' He smiled at her and she smiled back.

'Keeping the workers happy?'

'Something like that.'

She knew that the men in the team turned to him with their problems, that they got support and practical help every time. That was what she was getting and, as a girl, a shoulder to cry on. But they were still boss and team member. This was no man-woman situation and she mustn't make herself too comfortable in his arms, because her time limit seemed about a minute.

As he reached across to open her door she said, 'I think I'll go straight up to my room.'

She could do with an early night, a lot had been crammed into today. But Orme said quietly, 'I'd prefer it if you joined the others.'

That was his I-give-the-orders voice, quiet and calm but brooking no denial. He wasn't making a suggestion, he was telling her what to do. 'Why?' she asked.

'I don't want you sitting around on your own, mooning over Paul Mellor.'

She laughed at that. 'What a ridiculous idea!'

But it wasn't ridiculous, she might have done. 'I just feel like an early night.'

'You can still have one. It's only just after nine. Make it an early night at ten.'

An hour, spent with the rest of the team, should snap her out of the old dreams. They were good company, fun, and her friends. At ten o'clock she would be less likely to go sighing to bed.

'Orders are orders,' she said.

Orme said nothing, but as they walked across the car park into the inn he began to talk about tomorrow. Tomorrow Tessa had to do some sifting through reference books while the team were out, interviewing and filming. Orme was telling her again what he wanted her to look for, and she nodded and murmured, 'Yes . . . yes . . .'

The team had settled themselves in the corner they had chosen at lunchtime. Several of the locals were with them. No one Tessa knew, but everyone seemed friendly and there was almost a party atmosphere prevailing.

Orme and Tessa were hailed and Tessa was drawn in. Orme kept back. He was less of a party man than the others, and in a little while he was sitting in the background with a couple of older men, who were telling him their stories.

The TV team promised good business for the Stag's Head. Jimmy had been signing the autographs, his was the face the viewers knew, and the landlord and his wife were hoping this was going to last. A celebrity or two around the place should bring in the customers, and on winter's nights as a rule customers didn't exactly arrive in droves.

Margaret Baker had told Mrs Mann this evening, 'Some of them will be coming to see Miss Harris again, she comes from these parts.' So the landlady had a specially bright smile for Tessa, and passing Tessa, as she cleared a table, she asked, 'Any of your friends here?'

Margaret, thought Tessa; and wondered how much about her Mrs Mann had been told. She smiled, 'There was Jackie and Roger earlier, but this is only our first night. They'll be along.'

While she was here there were people she would like to see again. Her neighbours in the little row of cottages, girls she had gone to school with, the women she'd worked with in the supermarket.

But hers had been a restricted life. Her mother had died when she was a child, and although her father had loved her she had been 'keeping house' at an age when she should have been carefree. He was a serious-minded man, with a miner's stoop, and a miner's cough that killed him in his middle years.

Tessa had had no time to make friends. She was liked, and pitied, but occupied so that she missed out on youth, losing the girls who should have been her confidantes, the boys she should have dated. It was not until she left Blackstone that she had begun to make any real friends.

'Any of your friends here?' she had just been asked, and the answer she should have given to that was, 'I bought the best of them with me.' Among those who might come looking for her here were those who had laughed when her heart was breaking.

She whispered to Annie, 'I think I'll slip into the office, there are one or two things I'd like to look up for tomorrow. We don't want the men wasting their precious time, do we?'

'Slavedrivers!' Annie wrinkled her nose. 'All of them. See you in the morning, then.'

Tessa got out of the group fairly unobtrusively

and had a word with Orme in passing. 'Work,' she said. 'Ten minutes, then I'm having my early night. All right?'

'Goodnight,' he said. 'And no dreaming.'

She smiled. 'If I do it will be about tomorrow's schedule!'

There was no one in their office-cum-dining-room. She went to the table that was reserved for work, and opened her portfolio, going through papers and settling down with a list of places and times that had to be co-ordinated.

She was half way through a double check on that when the door opened and the landlady looked in to tell her, 'Miss Harris, there's a phone call for you.'

'Who is it?' Tessa asked, and Mrs Mann said, as though it was a virtue on her part not to inquire into guests' callers,

'I don't know I'm sure.'

'Thank you. Where shall I take it?'

'Along here. It'll be quiet in the office.'

Derek probably, thought Tessa. She had told him that Orme would be annoyed if he turned up at Blackstone, but there was nothing to stop him from phoning her. If it was Derek should she tell him she was 'engaged' to Orme? She knew that Derek was moving out of her life, but she would have preferred goodbyes without dramatics, and it might be best to sort things out there when she got back.

So she would simply explain that she was busy. Her working hours were the thing he was beginning to actively dislike about her, so this might be the final straw for him.

Bother Derek, she thought, and picked up the phone and said, 'Hello, Tessa Harris speaking.' Paul said, 'Tessa!'

'Who is it?' But she knew who it was.

'Paul,' he said. 'Are you alone?'

'Why?' She was sitting at a large old-fashioned desk that almost filled the cubbyhole of an office. The door was closed. She was quite alone.

'If there's anyone there,' said Paul, 'this is about that party I suggested throwing. Is there anyone you'd specially like me to ask?'

'No,' said Tessa. 'Except my workmates. Why the secrecy?'

'Are you happy?' asked Paul.

'Very,' she said.

'I'm not sure that I believe you.'

She should have laughed then, and proclaimed herself radiantly happy, and she did, but only after a hesitation that might have betrayed her. It was Paul's voice, of course. She must be sounding like a different girl, but his voice was the same and it brought back the things he had once said to her. Not the goodbye, although word for word that hadn't been harsh. Regretful rather, as though she had chosen to leave him, while his eyes showed blatant relief.

'Can I see you some time?' he said now. 'To talk to you?'

'Talk about what?' She held the receiver very tightly, pressed hard against her ear. She was tense and stiff, although she managed to sound relaxed.

'Old times,' said Paul, softly, gently, and she tried to laugh.

'I don't think Orme would care for that.'

'I don't much care about Orme,' said Paul, and that was foolhardy, when Tessa knew that Orme could make mincemeat of him. It didn't prove Orme the better man, much less the nicer, but Orme was stronger and vastly more intelligent, and in any conflict between them she knew that Paul wouldn't stand a chance. He must not antagonise Orme, he really must not.

She asked, 'Did you get a good look at my—fiancé?'

'I only saw you,' said Paul, 'for the first time in five years.'

That was how she had felt when he'd walked into the room. 'All the same,' she said, 'I think you *should* take a good look at Orme.'

'Does he object to you having friends?'

'Of course he doesn't.'

'We're old friends, aren't we?'

No, she thought, we are not. But pretending friendship was safer than admitting that their relationship had once been her reason for living. 'Of course,' she said.

'So why can't you come with me to look up some more old friends?' asked Paul. 'That's what you told my mother you were doing. Did you come to my home first?'

'Yours was about the nearest.' That wasn't even true, but she couldn't tell him why Orme had dragged her there. 'It sounds fun,' she said, although the last thing she intended doing was looking up old friends with Paul, or letting herself be drawn back into Paul's circle in any way.

'So we'll do that?' said Paul, and she prevaricated.

'Maybe, before I leave. But this isn't a holiday and my time off is limited—I'm working right now.'

'Where will you be tomorrow?' It sounded a casual query, but she didn't want him turning up to watch them. Orme would put out no welcome mat for Paul. 'Oh, here and there,' she said, 'and now I really must say goodnight.'

'Goodnight, then, and good filming.' He added

after the briefest of pauses, 'And I will be seeing you?'

'Of course,' she said. She put down the receiver and realised this was only the second time that Paul Mellor had phoned her. Once, at the very beginning, he rang her at the supermarket where there was a ruling against the staff having phone calls. When Tessa explained, and she hated explaining, he didn't ring again. She rang him, sometimes at his office, sometimes at home. She knew now what a nuisance she must have made of herself, and sympathised with the man at the receiving end. She had been very young, in every way.

But she remembered the joy of hearing Paul's voice on the phone, and an echo of it came back to her now so that she sat very still with a slight smile on her lips. Until she pulled herself together. No, she thought, *no*.

It was time she packed up work anyway. She went back and put her papers in a folder and the folder in the sideboard drawer that had been allocated to her. Then she hurried upstairs, hoping that no one would spot her.

Orme most of all. She didn't want him asking about that phone call. Mrs Mann must have inquired around to find where Tessa was, and in the morning, if he asked, Tessa would tell him,

But not tonight. Tonight she had done all the talking she intended, and all the listening too. Perhaps in the morning she would be good old Bones again, bright and efficient. Not Tessa, thinking of Paul who wanted to see her and talk to her, and wondering if she dared.

She was in bed, with the light off, when she heard Orme in the room next door. Faint sounds and only when you listened, but she knew he was there and she slid further down under the blankets, pulling a sheet over her head as though she was hiding from him.

It was ridiculous, but again she had the feeling that she was cheating, and that if Orme found out something quite terrifying would happen to her.

CHAPTER FIVE

BREAKFAST was always rushed and silent when the team was working. They all got the meal over as fast as they could get it down, and hardly exchanged a civil word until they were mobilised and ready to start work.

There was a standing joke in the TV company that Orme's team had to pass the breakfast test. If anyone was chatty at breakfast they could forget about getting into his team.

The first morning Tessa went out on 'field work' with them she came downstairs with a smiling good morning, and had her head bitten off by Freddie, who had growled, 'What's good about it?'

Now she knew better. Unless there was a major calamity to report she kept quiet until breakfast was over. This morning she hardly spoke to any of the men, because they were all off to film and interview men and women who were old enough to remember that day of fifty years ago when an explosion of fire damp had trapped all the miners in number three shaft behind a wall of fire.

Tessa was staying here, working in the office, and she really had no chance to tell Orme about Paul's phone call. If she had tried he would have told her to get her priorities straight. It could wait. She might tell him tonight.

When the men had gone she settled down with books and papers to work; and Annie, in scarlet hat and pants and short black plush jacket, and boots, looked in to say she was going into Blackstone and might catch a bus into Birmingham.

'Anything you want?' asked Annie.

'I don't think so.' Tessa put down her ballpoint pen and sat back in her chair. 'Are you looking for anything in particular?'

'Socks for Spike,' said Annie, 'although if I see a bargain for myself I might snap it up.'

Tessa smiled, 'Snap up one for me too.'

'You don't need to look for bargains now,' said Annie, and although she was happy for Tessa her expression was wistful. 'You'll be shopping where they don't even bother to put on a price tag.'

'Huh?'

'When you marry Orme.'

'Oh! Er—yes.' Orme's wife would have charge accounts, of course, with all the best houses. Most of the women he went around with looked as though they had already, as though they could have stepped out of the fashion pages of a glossy magazine. Tessa was surprised to find her thoughts so bitchy, almost jealous. She laughed and said, 'We're not married yet. I could be a working girl for a long time.'

'Will you go on working?' Annie had perched herself on the edge of the table and was all set to ask questions, and Tessa hastily picked up her pen.

'Of course,' she said. 'There used to be a bus to Birmingham on the hour and the half hour, but I don't know how they run now.'

'I can take a hint.' Annie slid off the table and made for the door. 'Like Spike says—that ring on your finger won't earn you any privileges if you get your facts wrong. Work comes first.'

Annie was not being bitchy, it wasn't in her nature, she was teasing, and Tessa laughed. But she didn't start writing again the moment she was alone. She sat for a few moments, looking at the ring as her hand lay still on the table. The ring didn't belong to her and it would be handed back to its rightful owner before long. But more than likely one day Orme would put a ring on some girl's finger that would mean they were going to spend the rest of their lives together. Would work come first then? she wondered. Would any woman ever take first place with him?

She didn't think so. He would be generous always, and kind and considerate up to a point, but she couldn't imagine him ever giving another human being any real power over him.

She thought—I wouldn't envy her, whoever she is. I shouldn't like to be the one who tries to handle him.

Then she did get down to work, because that was what mattered if she was going to earn her golden future.

She had interruptions. She had a phone call from a woman she had worked with, who was still a cashier at the supermarket, and had heard that little Tessa Harris was back. Tessa promised to call in the shop one day, and failing that to call round at Alice Lyons' home. She would do that. She would like to see Alice again.

Then Paul arrived. Nobody even came to tell her he was here, to ask if she would see him. If they had she would have said she was too busy and please leave a message, but he tapped on the door and when she called, 'Come in,' he did.

Her heart looped again. It always had when she'd looked at him, and it still did. She felt like a fan at a pop festival, palpitating at the sight of an idol. But she managed to sound slightly irritated. 'Oh, hello, what can I do for you?'

Paul took that at face value. He couldn't read her thoughts, or guess how she was feeling. He smiled apologetically. 'Sorry, may I come in?'

He was in, standing there beside her. Tessa looked down at her papers, then put down her pen with studied deliberation, and said, smiling, 'Sure, why not? What's it all about?'

He spoke abruptly. 'I wondered if you'd have dinner with me tonight.'

'You mean Orme and me?'

'I mean just you.'

She held up her ring hand. 'I am engaged. That means we try to do most things together.'

She had been right about needing a ring on her finger, although she still wondered if her fictitious vet would not have been safer for the part than Orme.

'But you're not married yet,' said Paul, and as her lips parted to say something—she had no clear plan what—he added huskily, 'I don't want you to make the mistake I made.'

This was becoming too personal and much too emotional. 'I'm sorry if you made a mistake,' she said quickly, 'but I see no connection.'

'You don't?' He tried to take her hand and she pushed her chair back, picking up a few papers and taking them to her sideboard drawer. 'Stella was suitable,' he said heavily, 'and we've bored each other to death.'

'Somehow,' she said, filing the papers which didn't need filing, 'I can't see Orme boring anyone.'

She could very easily see him infuriating anyone, but he had none of the negative qualities. You might want to murder him but never because he bored you.

'Why did you go away?' Paul asked softly, and she shut the drawer with a little bang, then faced him, smiling.

'Don't pretend you weren't glad to see me go.' Before he could speak she went gaily on. 'Now that *was* boredom setting in. I must have nearly sent you round the bend, phoning you, writing to you, following you about like a puppy dog.'

She came back towards her chair, and he moved forward so that she nearly stepped into his arms. But not quite. She halted, arms folded, and went on smiling. 'I had a blazing crush on you all right, but I'm grown up now. Older and wiser in the wicked ways of the world.'

'You came back,' said Paul, and she shrugged.

'I go to a lot of places. It's all part of the job.'

'But you're here now.'

'For three weeks.'

'Unless you decide to stay.' When he looked grave like this, and straight into her eyes, she felt like a callow girl again. Paul was asking her to stay, and five years ago that would have been offering her the keys of paradise.

When she'd told him she was leaving she had had a faint hope he might say, 'Stay.' Even when she was waiting for the early coach, in the almost deserted square, she had watched for his car to drive up until the very last minute.

She shook her head now. 'No chance,' she said.

But he went on looking at her, seeing a girl whose promise of being special had blossomed into something quite out of the ordinary. He wanted her back, and he believed he could get her. She had been crazy about him once, and he believed she would be again.

Tessa knew he was thinking that. She saw the confidence in his eyes and she still didn't know how she would react if he held her close, and kissed her hair and her eyes and her lips. She said, 'I have work to do, and I'm surprised you haven't.'

'I have.' But he still didn't move. 'I looked in to find out where you were this morning, and here you are.'

She moved past him to her chair, and sat down and picked up her pen and said, pointedly, dismissing him, 'Goodbye.'

'No, it isn't,' said Paul. But as she began to write he went, and as soon as the door closed she stopped writing. It had been gibberish anyway, and her hands were shaking so that it looked like an old woman's spidery script.

The magic was still there. It came back at her in waves and she could have sat around all morning, dreaming—like a retarded adolescent, as Orme would have said.

Orme would have a great deal to say if she didn't finish this lot before he saw her again, but it took much more effort than usual to clear her mind of everything but the work in hand. Paul came back, every time she relaxed her guard, so that the work was harder and by lunchtime she felt drained.

The tap on the door stiffened her. Not Paul again, please, but better Paul than Orme, although she couldn't have said why she dreaded seeing Orme.

It was Margaret Baker with a plate of sandwiches and a cup of coffee, the lunch that Tessa had ordered earlier. 'Thank you,' said Tessa, and asked, 'Any of them back yet?'

They'd expected to be out all day, but you never knew. Margaret shook her head. 'Not a sign. Nobody in the bar you know either.' She gave Tessa what could only be described as a funny look, as though she knew Paul had been here. 'Sandwiches are cheese and egg,' she said. 'The ham was on the fatty side, I didn't fancy it myself.'

'Cheese and egg will be fine,' said Tessa, and

when Margaret had gone she wondered why she hadn't said casually, 'Paul Mellor was in earlier. Did you see him?'

It was none of Margaret's business, but there was no need to make a secret of it. That would give a completely wrong impression. But somehow Tessa couldn't talk about Paul.

Not even to Annie. Annie arrived back late afternoon with several packages, and a gleeful glint in her eyes when she put her head round the door. 'Busy?' she carolled.

'I can call it a day.' Tessa got up stiffly, and stretched, looking at the packages and inquiring, 'What's in those?'

'Think I can show you before Spike gets back?' Annie decided she could and put her goodies on quick display. While Tessa was admiring a neat two-piece of skirt and waistcoat, navy, polka-dotted in red, Annie asked, 'How did your day go? Any excitement? Any visitors?'

'Slog, slog, slog,' chanted Tessa. She should have said, 'An old boy-friend of mine from way back dropped in,' but she didn't, and after the team returned the talk was work again.

They were really into it by now. All through dinner, and then, around the table, there was the evening conference, and Tessa concentrated on what everybody was saying so fiercely that her head began to ache.

For the first time being part of this high-powered organisation was putting a strain on her that was less challenge than ordeal. The adrenalin wasn't flowing as it should. She found herself drifting off into daydreams and when Orme, at the head of the table, bellowed at her she jumped in her chair.

'Well?' he demanded, and she had to mumble,

'Sorry, I didn't catch——'

They were all surprised. It wasn't like Tessa to lose the thread of a discussion, and Orme said in a silky voice that his expression belied, 'Do you think you might work up enough enthusiasm to get yourself round to the local newspaper office in the morning and check their columns on Will Stilgoe? You did hear who Will Stilgoe was, didn't you?'

'Yes,' she lied fervently. 'Of course I did.'

She hadn't heard a word for a good three minutes, but she knew that Will Stilgoe had been one of the heroes of the pit disaster. He had helped to bring out comrades who were overcome by fumes, and there was a faded photograph of him on the table, among the old photographs that would be used to illustrate some of the script.

'Are you all right, Bones?' Freddie was asking her.

They were all concerned. Tessa was looking flushed and confused, not her usual cheerful competent self at all. She really did have a headache, physically she was feeling very jaded. She said, 'I'm sorry, but I've got a headache.',

That was unusual too. Tessa very rarely complained of aches and pains, and Orme said, 'In that case you'd better go and lie down.'

He didn't sound as sympathetic as the others, and he was supposed to be the man who was in love with her. He had no time for play-acting at the moment, but she took him at his word because she was longing to get away, somewhere quiet on her own.

Did she want to be a career girl? Or did she want those early dreams to come true after all? She had changed into a girl of whom Mr and Mrs Mellor would no longer be ashamed. She was no longer the infatuated teenager whose naïveté had flattered and then bored Paul.

He was bored with Stella now, but without conceit Tessa knew she was brighter than Stella had ever been, and had worked much harder developing the talents she had. She wasn't prettier. Stella had a blonde ethereal daintiness, but Tessa didn't fear her as a rival.

Now if it had been Anthea Vella, she thought, or any of Orme's lot, that would be different. They were the big league, but she could meet anything Blackstone had to offer.

She didn't want to go into the bar, which was as full as last night when she passed through on her way to the staircase. But it was too early to go to bed, so she decided on a walk. She put on her fur coat and came downstairs again, avoiding looking around in case anybody signalled to her.

Outside the night was cold and clear and exhilarating. She had often walked across the hills as late as this. There wasn't much more light if she had kept to the roads. They were unlit, except for Greenheath Avenue, and even there the lamps were few and far between.

So she chose the track that crossed the hills, towards the Grey Lady, and beyond that to the church and the churchyard and the little row of cottages. She doubted if she would reach the pit, much less the cottages, but long before then the cold air should have cleared her head and maybe her mind.

The grasses crackled underfoot, she breathed deeply and stepped out, but almost at once she realised she was being followed, and stopped while she was still within earshot of the inn if she should have to shout for help.

Moorlands by dark could be hazardous, and the

mugging level had probably gone up here, as well as everywhere else, in the last five years. Of course whoever was behind her could have an entirely law-abiding reason for crossing the moors, but she came back towards the car park; and she didn't realise it was Paul until she was parallel with him.

Then he called 'Tessa!' and she whirled and stared, gasping, 'I didn't know it was you. What are you doing here?'

He came hurrying across. 'I was in the Stag's Head, I've been there for the past hour.'

She hoped he hadn't made his pursuit of her too obvious, or it would soon get around that Paul Mellor and Tessa Harris were starting up that old affair again. Not that she cared about local gossip, but Paul had to live with it.

'I think perhaps you'd better go back,' she suggested.

'Where are you going?'

'I was going for a walk over the hills,' she told him. The hills stretched away in the moonlight. 'But when I heard footsteps I decided it would be wiser to walk where the houses are.'

'You were walking alone? I thought you couldn't go anywhere without Orme Jared. Where is he to-night?'

'In conference.' She looked back at the lighted windows of the inn. 'They're all in conference. I'm getting some fresh air because I've been indoors all day and I need some air.'

She was trying to sound calm and casual when Paul said softly, 'I used to come this way to meet you.'

Then she looked with him across the moonlit track. 'One of the paths where ghosts walk,' Orme had said. Paul was still the man she had hurried to meet, but there might be a ghost of a girl out there somewhere, her early other self.

Although she was beginning to feel very young and vulnerable again, as though the two Tessas were merging, the past into the present. When Paul took her arm she let him, and they walked slowly together into the quiet hills.

'Do you still ride?' she asked.

'Not so much these days,' he said.

That was how she had seen him first, when she was about ten years old. It was the year her mother had died. Her mother had been ill for a long time, and Tessa had sat at the bedroom window reading to her, caring in every way she could—'a proper little nurse', the district nurse had called her.

She had thought Paul Mellor on horseback was like a prince, and he still was, on a night like this. Time stood still in this place where she had spent her childhood, and come to womanhood, dreaming her dreams.

She was young Tessa again. She asked a few questions, and Paul talked and she listened, and it was the same as it used to be. Even his opinions were the same, and she didn't disagree about anything.

When he turned to face her, and was obviously about to kiss her, she was awestruck. 'You haven't changed at all,' she said. 'It could have been last week, not five years.'

'Haven't I?' He smiled, pleased. 'Thank you.'

'It's incredible.' She shook off a sudden uncomfortable suspicion that it wasn't such a compliment. In five years he should have changed. In features he had aged very little, but he should have matured as a person, learned something more. He shouldn't be sounding exactly as he had sounded five years ago. The work she did and the company she kept had stretched her mind, and for a moment she felt the gulf between them.

Then he said, 'You've changed, you're more beautiful,' and kissed her, and that was as sweet as she remembered.

She closed her eyes and floated blissfully. Paul's arms around her, Paul's lips on hers, were what she had always wanted. But there was Stella; and there was a team of workmates back there in the inn whom she would be letting down if she let herself get carried away.

She couldn't go back to them and say, 'I've met my love again, so now you understand why I couldn't keep my mind on work tonight. Because I've regressed to adolescence—as Orme put it.'

At the thought of Orme she came down to earth with a bump, just at the moment Paul was whispering in her hair, 'I think I must have always loved you.'

Even when you were showing my letters around? she wondered. Even when you married Stella? But she said, 'We must go back.'

'And you've always loved me, haven't you?' He cupped her face in his hands, his handsome face just above hers.

'Back. Right now,' she gasped, and wriggled loose and began to walk fast.

'Silly little goose,' he said tenderly. 'Why are you afraid of me?'

'I'm not,' she protested, and Paul laughed at her and walked beside her, humouring her but more than satisfied with the situation.

She went back so fast that she was breathless when they reached the car park, and she had to stand for a few seconds before she could manage to say, 'Don't come in there with me.'

'Why not?' He was still laughing at her. 'Is Jared likely to beat me up?'

'I shouldn't think so,' she said. 'I've never seen him actually hit anybody, and he is a judo black belt, so maybe he pulls his punches.'

Paul stopped smiling. 'Is he?' he said. 'A black belt? Yes, well, perhaps not. But I'll be along to-morrow.'

Tessa said quickly, 'I promised to go round and see a friend tomorrow night. Somebody who used to work in the supermarket with me.'

'Friday, then? That party, the old gang, at my place?'

Orme had agreed to that when Paul suggested it last night, and she couldn't think of a good excuse. She nodded, moving away. 'Sounds lovely, yes. If we can't manage it I'll get a message to you.'

There were people in the car park, some coming, some going. She skirted them and didn't look back at Paul. She went round to the back door, but she still had to walk through the bar to get up the stairs and by now the conference was surely over. The TV team would be in there, and she didn't think much of her chances of getting upstairs without one of them spotting her.

She wanted to reach her room, as she had done last night, turn out the light and pull the sheet over her head, and she was half way up the first flight of stairs when Annie came dashing after her, squeal-ing, 'Bones!'

Tessa went on climbing, but slower so that Annie reached her, then she said, 'I've been for a walk, I thought it might do my head good.'

'Has it?'

'Yes, but I'm going to bed now.'

'Orme sent me up earlier to see how you were,' said Annie. 'Then the landlord told us you'd gone out. Sure you're all right now?'

'Fine, thank you, honestly.'

'Good,' said Annie, and went back down while Tessa went on up to the top floor and her bedroom.

So Orme had sent Annie up here. Orme knew that Tessa had gone out. Did he know that Paul had been in the Stag's Head and had followed her out? And what did it matter if he did? She could talk to Paul Mellor, or to any other man if she wanted. She could do whatever she liked with any other man. This engagement ring was a makebelieve. She was her own woman, accountable to no one but herself.

She slipped off her coat almost with a flounce, impatient with herself for skulking up here like this. Last night and tonight, acting as though she was scared of Orme.

'Why are you afraid of me?' Paul had just asked her when she had panicked and rushed back here, but it wasn't Paul she was scared of, it was Orme, and that was ridiculous.

In the morning she would tell Orme she had seen Paul tonight. She hadn't planned it, but she had seen him and they had talked, and she had an open mind about her future. It was possible she might be coming back to Blackstone sometimes. It was just possible that she might eventually marry Paul.

She couldn't say anything for certain, because she didn't know for certain, but she would see what happened and of course she wouldn't let what might happen reduce her efficiency. So long as she was part of the team she would work as hard as ever; and if she did resign she would give him plenty of notice.

She saw her reflection in the mirror of the dressing table, nodding approvingly at her sensible thoughts and reasonable attitude, and that made her smile wryly at herself. A split second later there was a sharp knock on the door and her reflection was suddenly wildly apprehensive.

'Who is it?' she called, after a few more seconds, looking at the closed door as though it might burst open.

'Orme.'

'I'm—in bed.'

'Then get out of bed and get this door open.' The knob rattled ominously. 'I've got a few things to say to you.'

She froze. From the sound of his voice he hadn't come to ask if her headache was better, and why had she said she was in bed when she was standing here fully dressed? She'd better cover herself with her bathrobe.

She snatched that up from the chair, and then tossed it towards the bed because he'd know she hadn't had time to get undressed. Could she say her headache was so bad that she had collapsed on the bed as she was? But she had just told Annie she was feeling fine.

Her thoughts were whirling, and she was hopping around like a scalded cat, when he called again 'Bones!' and she shrieked,

'Oh, for goodness *sake*!' and flew to the door and flung it open. 'What *is* it?'

He walked past her into the room, which took her breath and fanned her indignation so that her voice was fast and high. 'Look, all right, you're the boss. But this is my bedroom and I don't expect anyone to march in here unless I say so, and I don't recall asking you to step in.'

'Stop gabbling,' he said.

Tessa did talk quickly when she was nervous, and it didn't add to her dignity. From now on she would space her words when she meant to be cutting.

'I want to talk to you,' he said, 'and a bedroom's the one place where no one is going to disturb us.'

She blushed hotly, and instinctively put up her hand like a shield, trying to hide her discomposure. 'All right,' he said, 'sit down.'

He sounded as though he was conducting an interview and that annoyed her enough to swamp the embarrassment. She remembered to talk slower, with what she hoped was telling sarcasm. 'Thank you very much. Which may I take, my chair or my bed?'

Orme shrugged. Tessa went on standing, and he sat down in the chair himself. 'Now,' he said, 'what's going on? You saw Paul Mellor this morning, did you go out to meet him tonight?'

She wasn't standing here like the accused. She crossed to a small stool in front of the dressing table and sat on that, bolt upright and with her arms crossed. Then she said, 'May I say something before you start cross-questioning me?'

'Go ahead.'

She took a deep breath, slow-spoken and reasonable. She unclenched her fingers to show the ring, glancing down at it. 'I'm sorry I started this nonsense. I got worked up when I knew I was coming back here, but now that I've met Paul again I know I don't need protecting from him.'

'That wasn't the problem, was it?' Orme said mildly. 'So much as protection against yourself.'

'Well, yes.' She had been apprehensive of her own reactions, but this was just splitting hairs.

'What happened tonight?' he asked, and she knew

109

he wasn't going to be put off. He was going to sit here like judge and jury until she had answered all his questions.

The chair squeaked as he sat back. It was a pink wickerwork armchair and it was too much to hope it might collapse beneath his massive frame, but if it had done it would have made Tessa's day.

It didn't, and she said crisply, 'I did meet Paul just now. He was in the bar when I went out. I didn't see him. I didn't know he was there, but he saw me and went out after me and we walked around. And talked.'

Paul had talked. Paul always talked, he was no listener. Orme was a listener, eyes on her now, as though he followed not only what she said, but also what she left unsaid. And that could be very uncomfortable if you were trying to hold anything back.

Not that she was. She said defiantly, 'Very well then, I suppose I could still be in love with him.'

Orme shook his head slowly. 'No, you're not.'

'How do you know?' He might read her thoughts but nobody could read her heart. At least she hoped nobody could.

'Because you've grown up,' said Orme. 'You've grown away.'

She had felt that herself, just before Paul kissed her. He was attracted to the new Tessa, but he wouldn't want to listen to her, much less have her argue with him or oppose him.

'What did you talk about out there?' asked Orme, and she said,

'That is not your concern.'

He spoke as though she was missing an obvious point. 'But of course it's my concern, I don't want to lose you.' He wanted to keep her in his team, and if that was where her future lay at least she would never be bored. 'Where did you go?' he asked, so quietly that he sounded gentle.

'Over the hills. Towards the pit.' She was still sitting with tightly folded arms, and she hunched her shoulders now. 'It hasn't changed. Not in the moonlight. Nor has Paul. It was like stepping back into the past.'

'Was it?' She could hardly catch that, but he asked, 'Who phoned you last night?' clearly enough.

'Your spies must be everywhere! Paul.'

'Why didn't you tell me?'

She jumped up suddenly, her control of stillness snapping, jerking her about like a dancing marionette. 'I don't *know*. Why *should* I tell you?'

Orme was on his feet too, but he was still and his deep voice was calm. 'He's going to turn into a man very like his father one day, but I can't see you turning into a woman like his mother.' She had to grimace at that grisly destiny. 'That is not on,' said Orme.

It was not on, but it had been sweet when Paul had kissed her. She had floated beautifully until she remembered Orme and came down on hard ground.

She must have been looking dreamy again because he said, in the harshest voice he had used to her tonight, 'For God's sake wake up. Dreams are no substitute for living.'

There was no need of dreaming for him. He had the strength to take on life's challenges and enjoy them, and of course he had no patience with her dopey attitude. 'Do you reckon?' she said, and his large hands came at her in a threat that she hoped was mock, although he sounded exasperated enough to strangle her.

' I don't know whether to shake you or——'

'Or what?' she asked, without thinking, and his hands caught her shoulder blades, shaking her very slightly—or perhaps she trembled and thought he shook her—then drawing her against him and kissing her on the mouth.

She stopped breathing, her heart stopped beating. That was how it felt. For a blind moment body and mind ceased to function, and then she came alive with a jolt like a charge of electricity reaching every nerve. She had been kissed before, of course she had, but she had never before felt this piercing delight, not the wild exultant joy that could have blown every inhibition she had.

Her lips parted and her hands, flat against his chest, instinctively moved to reach up and hold him tight with all her might, so that she would be closer to him than she had ever been to any other living soul.

But somehow, from somewhere, she got the strength and the sense to push instead of cling, and as she did Orme loosed her. For a moment he looked at her, as though he waited what she would say. She said, 'What on earth do you think——' and he grinned.

'How did that compare with Paul Mellor?'

It had blotted Paul out completely, annihilating him. But she couldn't say that because that would be admitting that it had nearly annihilated her. She managed to shrug. 'You've had a wider experience, no doubt.'

'No doubt,' echoed Orme cheerfully. 'Haven't you?'

'I don't know,' she said, and then, indignantly, 'No, I haven't!'

He raised an eyebrow. 'You've always seemed to lead a varied love life.'

The team teased her about her boy-friends, but Orme had never shown any particular interest before. Although he soon would have done if they had interfered with her work, and she said,

'Too varied to get really involved. Men get fed up with the hours I work. And they're not too keen on me waltzing off for weeks at a time.'

'Hard luck.' But he laughed as he said it, he wasn't sympathising, and it hadn't mattered. Tessa hadn't wanted to get involved. There had always been that wariness from her early hurt from Paul. But the hurt was over now, and she said,

'It's nice to know you're sorry for me. Don't you have the same trouble?' Of course he didn't, and she answered herself. 'I suppose not. Success is fine for men, but for women it's something to play down.'

She was finding it disturbing to stand here, facing him, and she moved away to pick up her yellow towelling bathrobe from the floor and drop it on the bed. Then she went to the dressing table and stood with her back to him and announced, 'It isn't feminine to be too successful.'

'Nonsense!'

'Would you want a woman who was a success?' Again she spoke without thinking, and his reflection smiled at her.

'Am I being offered one?' Then he said, 'I know, the question is academic.'

What he didn't know, thank goodness, was that just now he nearly had been offered.

'The answer is—very much more than an unsuccessful one,' he said, 'although I can see that it might undermine Paul Mellor.'

For sheer strength of personality, allied with a cool and brilliant mind, it would be hard to find Orme's equal. Paul was no equal. Neither was Tessa, and she could understand why he would not feel undermined by anyone's success.

He said quietly, 'You're too talented to spend your life at coffee mornings with Mrs Mellor. It would be a criminal waste, and it would never make you happy.'

No, it wouldn't. It would bore her crazy. 'Neither would Paul Mellor,' said Orme. 'So he can't have you. I'll see to it.'

Tessa could have reassured him that it was all right, she was finally and completely free of Paul. 'I think it was what you just said about him being like his father,' she could have said, but instead she asked, 'How? What can you do?'

She still spoke to his reflection in the mirror, but the man stood behind her and that gave her a strange feeling of being surrounded by him, encompassed on all sides, a citadel under siege.

'Anything I have to,' he said, and a moment later, 'Goodnight.'

As soon as she was alone she moved fast, undressing, slipping on her bathrobe, along the corridor, in and out of the bathroom, and into bed. She gave herself no time for thinking until she was in bed, and then she relaxed and snuggled down, smiling.

She hadn't been quite honest with Orme, letting him think she was still undecided about leaving her job for Paul. But if she had convinced him there was nothing to worry about he would have stopped bothering. Once he knew she was a fixture again he'd let her go her own sweet way, and it would be much more pleasant to have Orme going with her for another few days.

That party Paul was arranging, for instance. She would love to take Orme along and introduce him to the girl who had told her they were all reading her letters. To introduce him to all of them. It would be very satisfying to meet them again with Orme, protective and possessive and stunningly attractive, by her side.

And not only when others were around. While he was keeping an eagle eye on her she would never have a dull evening. Orme was super company, and she would be a fool not to make the best of this opportunity for the rest of her stay in Blackstone.

When they left she would say that she wouldn't be coming back here, and she agreed absolutely that her future was with the team. That was what Orme wanted, the team intact, everyone working well together; and it was flattering that he was anxious enough to keep her to do anything he had to do.

Tessa wondered exactly what 'anything' meant. She was drifting into sleep now, and she turned her head so that she saw the connecting door glimmering lighter than the matt pink wallpaper. Orme was just the other side of that door, closer to her than anyone else in this building.

Tonight he had been much closer than anyone else. When Paul held her there had still been a gulf between them, but with Orme it had been a fusion. Her eyelids were closing, her limbs getting heavier, and she moved drowsily, her thoughts running uncensored and uncontrolled.

To keep her from Paul Orme might even make love to her. He had kissed her tonight, he might again. That would be highly unethical conduct, but the kissing had been an astounding experience that she wouldn't mind repeating. She smiled with eyes closed, remembering, and still smiling she slept.

CHAPTER SIX

TESSA spent the morning in the office of the *Blackstone Advertiser*, with a large bound volume of newspapers of fifty years ago. Will Stilgoe was her target, and she made notes on every mention of him she could find. About lunch time she came out again into present-day Blackstone, with her mind full of how the town had looked on the day the pit caught fire, and had to stand for a few minutes to adjust to modern times.

Then she headed for the supermarket where she had once worked. There was a new manager and the premises had been extended, but there were still a few familiar faces, Alice's among them.

Alice was a motherly little cottage-loaf of a woman, with a brood of children, most of whom were marrying and leaving home when Tessa left Blackstone. In the old days Alice's maternal instinct had extended to Tessa from time to time. Alice had always thought Tessa was too thin, and that it was hard on a young girl, being expected to look after first her mother, then her father, rather than being cared for herself, the way that Alice's own children were.

There sat Alice now, behind the till at one of the check-out points, and when Tessa said, 'Hello,' her round face wreathed in smiles.

'It's *Tessa*, and you're looking all right too. You didn't mind me ringing you yesterday, did you, but I was so surprised when I heard you were here, and I said, "I've got to see little Tessa Harris again".'

'I was thrilled to hear from you,' said Tessa. 'I'd have been down in any case. I wondered if I could come round to your house tonight.'

'Of course you can. Come and have a bite of supper with us.' Alice had spotted Tessa's ring and she beamed again. 'Is your young man here as well?'

'Er—yes, he is.'

'Bring him, then,' said Alice expansively. 'I'll make a steak and kidney pie.'

A customer plonked down a full basket and Alice began to ring up the purchases, smiling at Tessa between each item until Tessa said, 'Seven o'clock all right?' and made her getaway.

She would enjoy an evening with Alice, and however many of Alice's family were still at home; but she wasn't sure about asking Orme along.

She walked back to the Stag's Head, passing Paul's home without a qualm. That proved she was done with the old dreams. They were as distant as the old newspapers she had been reading, and less important.

Annie was in and the two girls ate lunch together, a thick meaty soup with new bread. Over lunch Tessa said, 'There's a party tomorrow night. We're all invited. You and Spike will come, won't you?'

'Of course we will,' Annie accepted promptly. 'What are you going to wear?'

'Oh, anything,' said Tessa, and then, 'Oh, well, I suppose I shall dress up.' She finished her soup, considering her limited travelling wardrobe, while Annie was doing the same.

Suddenly Tessa knew that she didn't want to be overshadowed by any of the other girls, and that wasn't because of Paul, nor to get her own back for old times' sake. It was because she wanted Orme to think that she was as attractive as any of them.

117

She worked during the afternoon, and then sat with Annie waiting for the men to come back. When Freddie walked in Annie got up to go and meet Spike, and she would have thought it odd if Tessa hadn't shown some enthusiasm. So Tessa walked out with Annie into the car park.

The three men were coming towards them, and as he saw her Orme began to smile. So did Tessa, instinctively quickening her step. 'How did it go?' she asked when she reached him.

'Very well. And you?'

'Mmm. Fine.'

They were talking of work, and yet somehow the questions had an undertone of personal concern. The others moved away and she stood there with Orme, and somehow she was in his arms, briefly, very casually. A quick hello hug, because she had more or less run out to meet him, nothing like as traumatic as the kiss had been, but immeasurably comforting.

They began to walk towards the inn, her hand slipped through his arm. The first time she had walked with her hand in the crook of Orme's arm had been only two days ago, and she had been ill at ease, awkward. Now she walked beside him, naturally close, and she thought—I like the feel of you more than any other man I have ever walked with.

Good grief, she thought, and swallowed and said, 'I've got a date for supper tonight. Alice Lyons, she was a cashier in the supermarket, and she's still there behind the same till.'

'Where does she live?'

'In the town.'

'Do you want a lift?'

She gave him a quick grin. 'I am going to Alice's. I'm not sneaking out to meet Paul.'

118

They were nearly at the door by now. Before Orme opened it he said, 'But you'd rather I kept away?'

'As a matter of fact you were invited.' She smiled mischievously up at him. 'Alice saw my ring and said I was to bring my young man.'

Orme chuckled. 'Not so young.'

'No?' She drawled with dancing eyes, 'But not so very old.'

Thirty-three, and her man, in theory, for what was left of this week and two weeks more; and although it was a fake it was an exciting thought.

As they went into the inn she told him chattily, 'Alice has six children. I don't know how many of them are living at home now, they're all grown up. And she's going to make a steak and kidney pie for tonight. If you come don't eat much, the pie should be good—she's a very good cook.'

'She'd need to be,' said Orme drily.

'She used to feed me sometimes. She'd sometimes bring a pastry along, or a little cake. She used to say I was skinny.'

He hung up his coat. 'You would have been,' he said.

The others were around the fire, but, although they stood in the fire glow too, it seemed to Tessa that no one could overhear or break into their talk. That was an illusion, but she felt alone, with just Orme.

She said, 'And that party Paul said he was giving, and you said you'd be delighted about. Well, last night I more or less said all right for tomorrow? Is it all right?'

'I wouldn't miss it for the world,' said Orme.

They took the car to get to Alice's. It was a cold night for walking, and by the time the evening meal and conference were over it was nearly seven o'clock.

As they passed the Mellors' Tessa murmured, 'I wonder where the next party will be. In the house or the new wing?'

Orme shrugged beside her. 'Does it matter?'

'Why should it?'

'Exactly.'

She wondered what she should wear, and who would be there. It was short notice. Paul would be hard put to round up all the old gang. Some must have left the district or even—like himself—have matrimonial troubles, which meant husband and wife couldn't both be asked to the same affair.

'Which way?' Orme asked, as they reached the roundabout in the town centre and her train of thought was abruptly broken.

'Oh, go straight across and turn right at the next traffic light. I'm sorry, I was——'

'Thinking about tomorrow night?' he said crisply. 'Don't let your expectations run away with you, you'll be heavily chaperoned.'

She made no reply to that. Instead she began to direct him in detail, watching the traffic, and generally acting as a conscientious navigator, to the gate of Alice's semi-detached house.

Alice was waiting for them. She came out and opened the gate and said, 'I *say*, that's a nice car.'

'It is, isn't it?' said Tessa, climbing out and coming round and hugging her. 'This is Orme,' she went on. 'I've told him about you.'

'That you used to feed her when she was a skinny child,' said Orme. 'I'm grateful to you.'

Tessa must explain some time that she wasn't hungry when Alice decided to feed her up, she was just naturally thin. There was always plenty of food in her own home, but Alice had a loving and giving nature.

The house was very warm and bright, and they were taken into a room where the table was laid for the evening meal and a red coal fire burned merrily in the hearth.

Alice's husband, Bernard, added his welcome to his wife's and that was all the family there was. All the children had gone, represented by photographs on the sideboard and the mantelpiece. Children, with spouses and grandchildren, all with smiling faces like Alice's and Bernard's.

Bernard was a small stout man, a good advertisement for his wife's cooking, and a postman by occupation. He and Orme shook hands, and it was not at all like it had been at the Mellors'. Bernard knew a lot about this area and Orme listened with genuine interest.

When Orme talked about his and Tessa's work he recounted the funny things that had happened, so that Alice laughed until tears rolled down her cheeks, and Bernard had a fit of coughing that necessitated him being thumped in the small of the back.

The evening was a great success, and the meal. As they ate Alice's steak and kidney pie Orme told her that Tessa had warned him to eat very little dinner at the Stag's Head because Alice's pie would be worth waiting for. 'And she was right,' said Orme, while Alice dimpled and blushed at his praise.

'You've got a good little cook yourself,' she said brightly.

'Have I?' When Tessa gave dinner parties the guests were well fed, but she had never invited Orme to a meal, and she looked up at him now through lowered lashes, controlling laughter. 'I'm gratified to hear it,' he said, but Alice was startled that the man Tessa planned to marry didn't even know she could cook.

She said earnestly, 'You've got a good little girl too.'

'I'm sure of it,' said Orme, and Tessa was suddenly acutely self-conscious, wondering what Alice was going to say next.

'Alice, please——' she began, but Alice was having her say, smiling approvingly at Tessa.

'She looked after her mother, nursed her when she wasn't much more than a baby herself. How old were you when your mother died?' Tessa shook her head, her hands gripped beneath the table. 'Ten, weren't you?' said Alice, having done her own calculating. 'Ten years old, and after that she looked after her father, did all the cooking and the cleaning.'

'Alice, *please*!' Tessa burst into this eulogy of herself as a small domestic paragon.

'Yes,' said Alice, 'all right, but it's nice to know you've found somebody who'll look after you for a change, because you're due for a bit of looking after.'

'I'm inclined to agree with you,' said Orme.

So who do you fancy for the job? Tessa might have asked him. She said, 'I can look after myself well enough. I'd hate to be looked after.'

'No, you wouldn't,' Alice contradicted her flatly. 'Not by the right man.'

Tessa was reminded of Mrs Prestcott, back at home, smiling when Orme took her out of the flats. Mrs Prestcott didn't know anything about this ring on Tessa's finger, but she had been fooled too, and Tessa was feeling ashamed of herself for deceiving Alice.

She wanted to admit—he isn't mine. Don't tell him about my past, because he isn't interested. It's the future he's concerned with, and for the future he's laying claim to my mind, not my body. He wants me as a colleague, perhaps as a friend, but in no way is he my lover, nor am I his.

Orme had kissed her last night, but that was impatience verging on anger, with maybe a soupçon of lust. It certainly was not love.

She insisted on helping Alice with the washing up and in the kitchen, with the door closed on the men, Alice went into raptures. 'Oh, you've got the right man there. He's a proper gentleman.'

'Is he heck?' muttered Tessa, too low for Alice to hear.

'I never did think that Paul Mellor was the right one for you.' Alice added washing up liquid to the bowl of hot water and gave it a brisk swish with the hand mop; and Tessa bit her lip, because of course everyone who had worked with her knew what a fool she had made of herself over Paul. That had been one time when she couldn't take care of herself.

'But it's all water under the bridge now, isn't it?' smiled Alice. 'When are you getting married?'

'We haven't decided.' Tessa picked up the steaming plates as fast as Alice deposited them on the draining board, as though in this way she could hurry this conversation to a close.

'You make sure of him,' was Alice's advice. 'You marry him quick.'

Tessa smiled wryly. If she had agreed that Orme Jared was an exceptionally good catch Alice would have been shocked at her cynicism, but that was exactly what Alice meant.

'I've got something to show you,' said Alice when

the last knife and fork had been replaced in the knife drawer and the towel draped over the stove to dry. She opened the door into the dining room. 'You go and sit down and I'll fetch it.'

Bernard had his stamp collection out and was telling Orme all about the stamps. The men had left the armchairs and were back at the table, so Tessa took an armchair herself and sat back and waited until Alice returned, carrying a large cut glass salad bowl which she put down on the table beside the stamp album.

'There,' she said triumphantly, 'what do you think of that?'

'It's lovely,' said Tessa, expecting to hear that Alice's husband or one of her children had bought it for her.

'It's yours,' said Alice. 'It's a wedding present.'

'Oh no!' Tessa looked appealingly at Orme, because this was next door to stealing, this was receiving under flagrant false pretences, and Alice's beaming smile faltered until Orme said in his deep cultured, undeniably sexy voice.

'How very kind of you. We shall treasure it.'

Tessa recovered quickly. Of course she couldn't refuse, she was ashamed of her ungracious reaction. The gift would be returned when the 'engagement' ended and that would be awkward enough, but right now she had to take it and look and sound delighted.

She said, 'It's beautiful, but you shouldn't,' and both Alice and Bernard insisted that they should.

'Now don't you forget to send us a piece of wedding cake,' was Alice's parting shot as the car moved away.

Tessa sat with the glass salad bowl on her knee. 'Don't take any corners at speed,' she begged Orme.

'If this falls off and breaks I'm in trouble. It has to go back when the engagement's called off.'

'Of course,' said Orme.

'I didn't expect to start collecting wedding presents.'

'That hadn't occurred to me either.' He chuckled in the darkness. 'They're a grand pair,' he said.

He had liked them much better than he had the Mellors. He was a good judge of character, but Tessa had always known that. She told him, 'Alice says you're a proper gentleman.'

'That's the tip of the iceberg,' said Orme.

Something else Tessa had always known, that the face Orme showed the world concealed a deep and complex nature.

'And she thinks I'm a born martyr,' she said. 'Do you?'

They were in the centre of the town, taking the road that would lead into Greenheath Avenue. 'On the contrary,' said Orme, 'I think you were born bossy,' and Tessa gave a little gurgle of laughter.

'That could be. I didn't mind running the house for my father, it wasn't that great a hardship.'

'All the same, you were very young to be pitched into responsibiltiy.' She felt him looking at her, and wondered if he was seeing her as a skinny child. 'Ten years old when your mother died,' he said quietly. 'That was a bad age for a girl to lose her mother.'

She spoke softly, almost to herself. 'What could be a good age?' The question sprang naturally from her lips. 'How old were you?'

'Fourteen.'

'Both of them?'

'Yes.'

Fourteen would have been a bad age. What was

Orme like at fourteen? What would he be like in forty years?

I wish I knew you better, she thought, more than the tip of the iceberg. She would be into deep waters then, and she sat quiet and still, half afraid he might read her thoughts.

They were nearing Paul's house, passing it when he asked her, 'Do you have any other family?'

'No. You have, haven't you?'

'No brothers or sisters, but relations.'

'Who brought you up?' In the last few days he had had a crash course on her, so why shouldn't she ask him a few questions?

'My father's parents,' he said.

'The admiral?'

'Yes.' The admiral was dead but from the way he said that one word Tessa know that Orme had loved the man and had rich and rewarding memories of him.

'I've heard of your grandmother,' she said, and he laughed.

'Who hasn't?'

'She must have been very beautiful.'

'She is beautiful. God knows how it's happened, but at eighty-four she is still beautiful.'

'Are you proud of her?'

They drew up in the car park, but neither made any move to get out of the car. 'I am,' said Orme. 'Do you mind if I smoke?'

'Of course not.'

He took out a thin cigar from a pack in an inner pocket of his coat. He didn't often smoke, but Tessa was glad he wasn't hurrying in, that he wanted to sit out here with her for a while longer. He used the car lighter and when the cigar glowed she said, 'And of course she's proud of you.'

Success was all very well for its own sake, but to have somebody caring about everything you did must be wonderful.

'Not particularly,' said Orme. 'I've disappointed her so far.'

'I can't believe that.' What did Lady Ursula want from her grandson? He was brilliant, famous, right at the top of his chosen profession.

'Thank you.' In this filtered moonlight his face looked like a carved face with darkness for eyes, and strong curved mouth, magnificently masculine. There was also a faint smell in the air of aftershave which, Tessa decided, combined potently with cigar smoke.

'What *does* she want?' she demanded, and he said lightly,

'Films don't impress her. She wants a production with more far-reaching consequences. A great-grandchild.'

'That's natural enough.' Most women wanted children, grandchildren, and if they lasted that long great-grandchildren; and in a woman with Lady Ursula's family tree there would be family pride as well, the instinct to preserve the unbroken line and hold the future in her arms.

But it seemed that the dynasty instinct wasn't in Orme or he would have been married by now, begetting sons. She asked, 'So why don't you give her one?' and he turned with a wicked glint.

'Can I rely on your co-operation?'

'Don't be daft!' She was glad the light was dim because she flushed agonisingly as he said,

'For a moment I thought this was going to be the good turn you offered to do for me yesterday.'

Her offer of what she would do for him some day, when he was dragging her up to the Mellors' front door, had been a threat, not a promise. He was joking, of course, and she said, 'Very funny, count me out, but I should have thought you'd have managed to find someone who'd oblige among all your ladies.'

He drew on the cigar, his tone as bantering as hers. 'You make it sound as though I'm running a harem! My trouble is that my grandmother has one old-fashioned condition. She wants her great-grandchildren to be legitimate.'

And he didn't want to marry. 'Tough,' said Tessa. 'They travel faster who travel alone. If it's speed you're after rather than the patter of tiny feet.'

She was chattering too quickly again because she was uneasy, although of course she wasn't really being propositioned. One day Orme would marry and Lady Ursula would get her stake in the future. But that would not concern Tessa, and a painful feeling of isolation was spreading through her for all her forced flippancy. She didn't understand it, but she knew she was miserable. She said, for talking's sake, 'She sounds rather splendid, does your grandmother. A genuine matriarch. I'd like to meet her.'

'You see that car?' Orme pointed towards the inn. 'The grey Rolls.'

'Who could miss it?' said Tessa.

'That,' he said, 'is my grandmother's car. As soon as we walk through that door you'll be meeting her.'

'*What*?' She jumped so that the cut glass bowl slithered off her knee and she was too startled to grab for it. 'You mean she's *here*?'

That was what he meant. That was what he had just said. Lady Ursula Jared had never turned up before when they were working, although she sometimes graced award presentations with her presence. Tessa had never met her, and it was surely more than coincidence that had brought her here tonight.

She held out a shaking hand, asking in a shaking voice, 'What about this? Does she know I'm wearing her ring?'

'I told her I'd borrowed it,' said Orme. 'I phoned her last night.'

'What did she say?' She was having visions of an indignant Lady Ursula demanding the return of her property, but Orme said blandly,

'She was delighted,' and then, 'She took it for granted that you're marrying me.'

Tessa gasped, 'Why did you let her? You should have explained that it wasn't a real engagement.'

'That kind of explanation would have been rather complicated,' he drawled, so calm that she could have beaten against him with clenched fists. Her nerves were screaming against the inquisition that faced her.

'So is this complicated.' The words were coming so fast that they fell over each other. 'So she's come down here to look me over? Well, I'm certainly going to enjoy that! I couldn't even pass the Mrs Mellor test, so how do you reckon I'll make out when Lady Ursula starts on me?

'You can talk about the tip of the iceberg—well, you're not alone. My tip of the iceberg is the way I look and the way I talk and the way I act these days, but only a mite beneath the surface and I'm the skinny kid that Alice thought needed feeding up, and I could well start babbling in the accent that used to have Mrs Mellor shuddering over her coffee cup. Broad Black Country. I'm not going in there to be catechised, I can tell you. Wild horses wouldn't get me in there.'

Orme had lowered the window and dropped out

his cigar. Suddenly he gripped her shoulders like a vice, holding her facing him. She had been jigging around, but now she had to sit still in her seat.

In his deep slow voice he said, 'How do you do it? Rattle on without drawing breath. Now shut up, and take a good deep breath and listen to me.'

Tessa tried to speak again, but his was the stronger voice. 'She'll like you,' he said. 'That is going to be the difficulty. She is going to take to you so that when I have to explain that the engagement is off I'm going to have more trouble with her than I anticipated.'

She thought she understood. 'You mean she's so anxious to see you married she'd take to any girl you brought along?'

'God, no!' The deep chuckle almost made her smile, although she supposed that was because she was darn near hysterical. 'You should hear her on some of them,' he said. 'Come to that, you probably will if I let her stay around here any length of time, so I'll see to it that she goes in the morning.'

Tessa didn't understand. She asked in bewilderment, 'But why should she like me? I'm not her sort.'

He wasn't holding her hurtfully now. His touch was almost gentle and so was his voice. He said, 'You have spirit and style and courage. You're made to measure, exactly her sort.'

Tessa's lips parted and she held her breath. For a moment she had thought he was going to add, 'And mine,' but he didn't. That was all he was saying, but those were compliments enough, goodness knows. She relaxed, cheered and comforted.

Of course she knew he was saying this to boost her confidence so that she would not make an idiot of herself in front of them all, after her threat of screaming hysterics. She smiled slowly, shaking her head at herself but in control of herself now. 'Nothing like a bit of flattery, is there?'

'That's not flattery,' said Orme, smiling too. It was, but she hoped she had spirit and courage and, on the surface at any rate, style. 'Shall we go in?' he said, and she stooped to pick up the salad bowl. It seemed to be all right.

He reached across to open the door for her, telling her, 'I felt you should be warned she could bring up the subject of great-grandchildren.'

He had spotted the car as soon as they had entered the car park, and Tessa was prepared now to be viewed by Lady Ursula as the prospective mother of Orme's sons. No, she wasn't. She would blush from head to foot, but she did know what was coming, and it wouldn't be easy for Orme either.

'Talk about tangled webs,' she said as she got out of the car. 'I hope you're going to think this masquerade is worth all this trouble in the end.' It was cold after the warmth of the car, but it wasn't the chill of the winter's night that made her shiver so much as a darkness of the mind. She heard herself say, 'However it ends,' because, suddenly, she couldn't see ahead.

'I know how it's going to end,' said Orme, quietly and grimly.

'Do you?' The way he wanted, with things as they were before the TV team came to Blackstone. But for Tessa that might not be possible. Too much had happened, and was happening to her. She had slipped into a whirlpool. She was being buffeted and tossed so that she didn't know whether she was coming or going, and even if she did eventually end up in calm waters she would never be quite the same again.

There was an almost full house in the Stag's Head. They walked in, unnoticed by most of the customers, including the group in the corner where Lady Ursula was holding court.

She sat in the largest high-backed armchair, with a footstool. She might have been tall once, but now she was tiny, doll-like. She wore a high-necked purple jersey dress, half a dozen or so long thin gold chains around her throat, and the rings flashed on her fingers. Her hair was still dark, when she was young it might have been raven, and her skin was translucent, and almost unlined. She had a heart-shaped face with high cheekbones, and Tessa said softly, 'She is very beautiful.'

'Look at her,' said Orme. Everyone around was looking at her, not only the team but half the customers. She was holding court, enchanting them all. He said, 'She'll charm ducks off water if she wants them on dry ground.'

'It runs in the family,' murmured Tessa drily. He had her arm and he gave it the slightest of shakes.

'Are you suggesting I always want my own way?'

'Every time,' she said. He grinned.

'But I've got some good films to show for it, haven't I?' and that made her laugh.

They made their way across and Tessa glimpsed Lady Ursula's expression as she got her first sight of Orme, towering over the heads, coming towards her. Her face lit with joy. There was an ebony cane, with a silver knob and ferrule, propped up beside her, and she reached for it, pressing her other hand down on the arm of her chair, striving to rise. But Orme reached her and supported her, reseating her. Then he asked, 'Why didn't you tell me you were coming?'

She had a clear voice, each syllable enunciated like an actress's voice. Nice voices, thought Tessa, they both have nice voices. Any actor would be happy to sound like Orme. 'A late afternoon impulse,' said Lady Ursula Jared. 'And I wanted to surprise you.'

She looked from Orme to Tessa, from very blue eyes. When she was young she must have been heartbreaking.

'And you wanted to meet Tessa,' said Orme.

'Of course.'

Everybody was watching them. Tessa stood rigid, clutching her salad bowl, and Orme turned to Mrs Mann, the landlady, who was standing a little way away, to ask. 'Does she have a room?'

Mrs Mann bustled forward, smiling. 'She's having ours, my husband's and mine. There's the sitting room too. Just for the night.'

Of course, thought Tessa. It seemed Lady Ursula was leaving tomorrow, so there was just tonight to get through.

Orme asked, 'Is it ready?'

'Yes, sir.'

'Then we'll see her up,' he said, and to Tessa, 'Come on, darling.'

She had never heard him call anyone darling before, not even on the telephone, although he must have used the endearment in private. He hardly had a harem, but he was never without a lady. It would be amusing to hear Lady Ursula's mimicries. Tessa wondered if she did Anthea Vella, if Miss Vella had heard about the 'engagement'.

Lady Ursula had a hand through Orme's arm and her cane for support too. Tessa paused to hand over the salad bowl to Annie, asking her, 'Could you put that somewhere for me?' She really couldn't

133

bring up the procession carrying this great bowl in front of her.

'Sure,' said Annie. 'Oh, a man called Paul Mellor came in about the party tomorrow night. Eight o'clock.'

'Fine,' said Tessa.

'He's very good-looking, isn't he?' said Annie. 'And——' she began, when Orme turned his head and she changed her mind and shut her mouth. Tessa would have to wait to hear what Annie had been going to say next.

The rooms were on the ground floor, a small parlour leading into a bedroom. There was a fire burning in the parlour, and a sofa towards which Lady Ursula made her way, and on to which she lowered herself slowly.

Mrs Mann had accompanied them and Lady Ursula said, 'My nightcap now, please. Miss Burton will tell you how I like it.' Off went Mrs Mann to consult Miss Burton. Companion? Lady's maid, chauffeur? Tessa wondered, and wondered where— Miss Burton was sleeping tonight.

As the door closed Lady Ursula tapped the far end of the settee with her wand of cane, like the good fairy or the wicked witch, and said, 'Now sit down and let me look at you.'

Tessa sat bolt upright, horribly conscious of being assessed on her chances of producing healthy offspring. 'Yes,' said Lady Ursula, 'I can see now how you get your nickname "Bones". Your workmates call you that, don't they? and I thought it was an ugly name to call a young girl, but now I see why.'

Tessa supposed she must be looking haggard, she wished Orme would explain, but Lady Ursula went on, 'Beautiful cheekbones, good bone struc-

134

ture You'll last. You'll make a very presentable old woman. You're like me, my dear.'

'Oh!' gasped Tessa, realising that she had just received the ultimate compliment, although she hadn't been nicknamed for her inner beauty.

Orme said, 'I prefer Tessa.'

He was the one who had called her 'Our Miss Bones' in the first place, but she didn't mind what he called her. 'Darling' had been nice, she thought, and hid her smile.

'We don't really need you, Orme,' said his grandmother, and Orme said,

'I'm sure you don't, but I'm staying.' He drew up a chair and settled comfortably into it. 'And we'll give you fifteen minutes,' he said. 'Then it's time you were in bed, and we've got a full working day tomorrow.'

She didn't argue. She said, 'Yes, of course, and I'm leaving in the morning, but the first weekend you have free Orme must promise to bring you to Midwinton.'

That was her home in Gloucestershire. 'I'll do that,' said Orme.

He wouldn't, thought Tessa. He would delay, then explain that they had called off the engagement. She remembered a photograph in a magazine somewhere of the old house, and thought, I would like to have seen Midwinton, I would like Orme to have taken me there.

Mrs Mann tapped the door and entered with a glass of what looked like very creamy hot milk. Lady Ursula tasted and nodded approvingly. 'Just right. Thank you. Hot milk with a spoonful of honey and a dash of whisky,' she explained to Tessa, and in the next breath, 'Now tell me all about yourself.'

'I——' Tessa looked helplessly at Orme. What did he want her to say? Where should she start?

He said, 'Tessa was born in this town. She lost her mother when she was a child, her father when she was seventeen. She nursed her mother and she kept house for her father. She also held down a full-time job until she left here at eighteen. Now she works with me, and she's a quite exceptional lady.'

Tessa wondered if Lady Ursula noticed that he did not say, 'I love her.' It would have been untrue, but not saying it might seem suspicious, and his grandmother looked steadily at him in silence for a few seconds. Then she smiled and said,

'I'm very happy for you both.'

Tessa thought—I hope you won't be too unhappy when you find those great-grandchildren are as far away as ever. I hope Orme gets himself genuinely engaged quickly, and married, and——

She flinched from that. No, I don't, she thought. No ...

Those two were fond of each other. In this little room there seemed to be a magic circle around the fragile old lady and the powerful man. It showed in many ways. As Orme took the empty glass from his grandmother, as her eyes followed him to the table and back to his chair, Tessa saw her pride in him, his tenderness for her. His protection was what kept her youthful in old age.

Beautiful bones weren't the answer. She had had a loving husband and she was still loved. Sitting on the edge of the settee, Tessa felt a physical ache to reach out and touch Orme, as though her nerve ends cried for the pressure of his hand. She was alone, incomplete, twisting the ring that would never belong to her.

But the inquisition she had dreaded wasn't an

inquisition after all. Lady Ursula didn't ask her any personal questions, and she was thankful for that, because the old woman had a cutting tongue. It was easy to imagine her handling those she disliked quite wickedly.

She didn't shut Tessa out. She talked as though the people she was discussing would become Tessa's friends, or bore or amuse her in the years to come. She trotted out sharp little vignettes about a procession of people, while Orme listened tolerantly and Tessa thought—if I ever did meet them I bet I could recognise them. I wonder how she'll describe me when she gets her ring back and hears that she's seen the last of me.

When Lady Ursula asked about the film they were making in Blackstone Tessa answered some of her questions. And when she said, 'Is it going to be worth watching when you've finished it?' Tessa said hotly,

'Of course it is, any film Orme directs is the best.' She finished lamely, 'Everybody knows that,' and with the smile that made her look young and pretty Lady Ursula said,

'I'm sure they do.'

Orme put a hand on Tessa's shoulder and smiled at her, and suddenly she was inside the magic circle and it was as though they both loved her. She had needed Orme to touch her, and now she looked into his eyes and wanted to kiss his mouth.

A long time ago, four days ago, he had said something about a bolt from the blue. Maybe it was as sudden as that, but the knowledge seemed deep and sure as a pulse beat inside her ... I want Orme. I want his children. I want him to have no woman, no wife, but me ...

CHAPTER SEVEN

LATER, when she was alone, and the lights were out and she was laying in bed, Tessa wondered how long she had felt this way about Orme. It didn't seem new. It was as though something had been staring her in the face for ages and she had never noticed it before.

She had always admired his work, the way he handled challenges, difficulties, life. She had always known he was attractive, you only had to look and listen to know that. There had been antagonism. No one could make her angrier, which meant there was no one of whom she was more aware, right from that first day when she went up to his office to take that dictation.

Beneath the outgoing ease of manner he was the most reserved member of the team. But when she had looked at him tonight and thought—I am in love with you, it had come as no surprise.

Of course I love you, she had thought, that's why I am still playing this game of makebelieve, because it keeps you near me.

But the 'engagement' was makebelieve, so did this mean she had to have a hopeless passion? As soon as the golden idol of her childhood crumbled was she building another impossible dream? Was she a born dreamer, in perpetual flight from reality?

No, she was not. And Orme was not the stuff of which dreams are made. He was too abrasive, too exasperating, much too alive. 'For God's sake wake up,' he had urged her. 'Dreams are no substitute for living.'

She wasn't dreaming now. She knew what she wanted from life, but she knew that the chances of his feeling the same way were remote.

'So long as we're in Blackstone I'm the man in your life,' Orme had said, the night Tessa told him about Paul. Well, she was the girl in his life so long as they were here, and she wouldn't think of the kind of competition she would be up against when they left. She'd meet that when she had to.

Tonight, for the first time, she hadn't taken off the ring and put it on the dressing table. She was still wearing it, and there was enough moonlight for it to glimmer faintly when she moved her hand.

Wish on a star, they said. You must stand a better chance if you carried your star with you. She kissed the wandering star that was her ring, and wished on it . . .

Next morning, as the team was leaving for the day's filming, Annie got a moment with Tessa and told her, 'Derek rang last night. I spoke to him and he said he was thinking of coming down.'

That had to be stopped, of course. Tessa would have to phone Derek the first possible moment about that.

Annie said, 'He didn't know you were engaged, did he? Have I been horribly tactless? I just blurted it out.'

Tessa was wrapping her scarf around her, over-coated and booted and carrying her clipboard and papers, as she walked through the main lounge to get into the car park. 'I hadn't got round to writing to him,' she said, 'but I'm sure it didn't worry him too much.'

'He didn't seem all that surprised,' Annie admit-

ted, and giggled. 'He said you never could stop talking about Orme anyway.'

'Did he?' Tessa stood stock still. 'I suppose I do
talk about the job quite a lot, but I didn't realise I
talked about Orme all that much. Do I?'

'Looking back on it,' Annie mused, 'now I know
how things are, I suppose I ought to have realised
you fancied him.'

The men had gone out to the cars, Tessa had
been trailing behind when Annie hissed her in-
formation about last night's phone call. But now
Tessa had to stop to ask:

'Did you—ever think he could be fancying me?'
and Annie said cheerfully,

'No, never. But that's his ring you're wearing,
and he's keeping tabs on you these days, isn't he, so
he must more than fancy you.'

The outer door opened and Orme glared in.
'What kind of conference is this? Come on, I
thought you were just behind me.'

Annie fled into the warmth of the inn, and
Tessa scurried out into the cold towards the cars.
Orme was keeping tabs on her all right, but his con-
cern could be strictly professional.

They spent the day with Will Stilgoe's son, a
spritely sixty-eight-year-old, who had been working
in the lamp shed fifty years ago. His reminiscences
were vivid and detailed and tied in with other
men's memories that were already preserved on
tape and film.

After midday Tessa came back to deal with paper
work. She washed her hair, and pinned it in, and
sat with a towel round her head, working busily.
Annie had an advantage, time to go to one of the
town's hairdressers in honour of the party tonight.
She took a taxi back to preserve her short fine fly-

away hair in the pretty cap style, and presented herself to Tessa to ask, 'Do you think I look soignée?'

Tessa grinned. 'Is that what you're after?'

'A new image.' Annie struck the dramatic pose of a high fashion model, and Tessa adjusted her turban of towel.

'Aren't we all?' she said.

'Shall I blow-dry you?' Annie offered, and brought down her hand hair-dryer and stood behind Tessa, drying her hair while Tessa finished her work.

By the time the men returned both girls had their party hair-do's. But as the styles hadn't changed drastically since this morning—just shinier and bouncier from the shampooing—none of the men noticed.

The evening meal was eaten, the conference got through, and at about half-past seven Tessa went upstairs to get ready. Annie was wearing her new polka-dot skirt with a scarlet sweater, and this was an impromptu party, so anything pretty and gay should do.

Tessa wanted it over. She would be the target of prying eyes, and the more she considered that the more reluctant she became to put herself on display. She chose her pink silk shirt, with a long dark red velvet skirt, and sat in front of the dressing table brushing her hair. It fell into natural waves and brushing usually soothed her. But tonight nothing did. She was ready but stiff and tense when Orme tapped on the door and called, 'Ready?' Instead of getting up and going she called back,

'Yes, come in.'

He was wearing a velvet navy jacket, black trousers and a pale blue lawn shirt, and Tessa put down her brush, with a little bang on the dressing table, as he came into the room and stood looking across at her.

'Who will we be meeting tonight?' he asked. She shrugged slightly and it was almost a shudder.

'Paul's friends. None of them were mine.'

'Do you want to go?'

If she said no he would help her think up an excuse, but how could she stay away after letting things go this far? 'I don't have much choice,' she said. 'Annie's looking forward to it for one.'

'Who's stopping Annie from going? I'm asking you.'

She got up, slowly picking up her fur coat from the bed. 'I'll survive,' she said as he held the coat for her. 'Just stay by me.'

'Why else do you imagine I'm going?'

As the warm light coat settled on her shoulders she relaxed enough for a smile to start. 'Do I look all right?' she asked him anxiously.

'Sensational.' Her eyebrows rose, her wide dark eyes widened even more. She knew that she didn't look sensational. In spite of the blusher on her cheeks she looked pale and strained. 'It's the blusher of course,' said Orme solemnly, tracing them with light forefingers, warming her skin with his touch. 'Superb bone structure is not given to every woman.' He surveyed her with smiling eyes in a mock grave face. 'You and my grandmother have a great deal to be thankful for.'

She smiled easily then. Lady Ursula had left this morning. There had been a note for Tessa when she returned, reminding her of her promise to visit Midwinton on her first free weekend. She wondered if Orme had been reminded too. She said, laughing, 'It's nice to know I'll make a presentable old woman.'

'More than presentable,' he assured her. 'A witch at any age is spellbinding.'

'Are you calling me a witch?'

'Of course.'

Her mouth went down in a grimace, then upped in a grin. 'Pity it isn't a fancy dress, we could have gone as a witch and a giant.' Even in her enveloping coat Orme dwarfed her when he was this close, so that she felt very small and right now very feminine.

He chuckled. 'Or, more obviously, as Beauty and the Beast.'

Anything that made a pair would be right by Tessa. She wished she could have said that, but she couldn't. She said gaily, 'I don't know what kind of party this is going to be, but if Mrs Mellor has anything to do with it there'll be plates of petits fours all over the place. Mrs Mellor was famed for her petits fours.'

'I'd rather have Alice's steak and kidney pie,' said Orme.

'I cook a good pie myself.' She went on smiling, making light of an invitation that had implications. 'Would you care to try one some time?'

Annie appeared in the open doorway, and said, 'Oh!' seeing them both, and then, 'Are you coming?'

'We're with you,' said Orme, and to Tessa, 'Yes, to the pie.'

Annie blinked at that, and Tessa slipped her hand into the crook of Orme's arm. 'They'll all be five years older,' said Tessa, 'but I'll probably have changed the most.'

The party was being held in the annex, in the home that had been built for Paul and his wife. Cars were filling the drive and the annex front door was open as a couple went in. The TV team arrived together, getting out of their two vehicles and moving en masse up the drive to the door.

I'm arriving well supported, thought Tessa. I'm bringing my champions with me.

She was the first to step over the threshold as the door opened again, Orme beside her, the rest crowding close. Paul had opened the door and he said how glad he was they had come, how much everyone was looking forward to meeting them. Somebody took coats away, into a little cloakroom leading off the entrance hall, and they were ushered into a room that stretched practically the whole width of the annex.

Paul's home was a follow-on of his parents' life style. The furniture was modern here, all carefully chosen to stand in its selected place. None of your cheap-and-cheerful, expensive but somehow characterless.

On the table and the long low sideboard was a catered buffet. Tessa knew the shop the cakes and savouries had come from, she recognised the selection. There was no sign of Mrs Mellor, nor her petits fours. This was the young generation of Blackstone, but not as young as they used to be. Five years more settled in their looks and their ways, and all of them here to see Tessa.

There was silence as she walked into the room, and they turned to stare at her, and she wondered what they were expecting. She had been a joke to them in the old days, following Paul like a puppy dog, sending him those passionate, ridiculous letters.

They had all seemed so sophisticated and brilliant to her then. But now she looked at them and they were ordinary. There was nothing exceptional about any of them. They looked pleasant enough, probably kindly, and rather on the dull side.

The exciting men were with Tessa, and Annie could have matched any girl here. Jimmy was the well known face, and Orme the international name.

Paul said to Tessa, 'Well, you know everyone here, so welcome home.'

You have got to be joking, thought Tessa. Meeting Orme's impassive gaze, she said, 'I'd better introduce you.' She recognised most of the faces, they all looked eager to meet the celebrities, but she realised at once that she couldn't guarantee putting the right name to every face. So instead she presented the team, 'Annie, Spike, Orme, Jimmy, Freddie,' and gave everyone a smile, suggesting, 'Supose you all introduce yourselves.'

The team moved in and the party took off and it could have been a real ego trip for Tessa.

The impact she was making on the men was very flattering. They thought that the five years since she was last under the Mellor roof had done wonderful things for her, compared with the girls who had stayed put. As for the women, they envied her.

Some tried to hide it by being very carefree and casual. Others were open about it, saying that her job sounded fantastic, wanting to know about the famous people she had met, looking at Orme with expressions that said, 'All that and him too?'

Orme was the main reason they all envied her. Not only who he was, but because he had an arrogant sex appeal that made him the most attractive man in that room. And Tessa was wearing his ring and he was beside her most of the time. Even when they were apart his eyes kept track of her.

He was, of course, making sure she didn't succumb to Paul's blandishments. There was no danger, but Orme didn't know that. Nor did the rest of the company know why he watched her.

Paul was drawn irresistibly to Tessa. In spite of that walk across the hills, when he had believed he could catch and hold her again, he knew now that she was out of his reach. But he never left her, and whenever Orme moved out of earshot Paul's voice dropped caressingly low.

Not that he said anything compromising—the room was full, others might have overheard. As it was they must be aware that Paul was getting the brush-off this time. But when he handed Tessa a glass of punch, with Orme across the room, talking with some of the men, and briefly no one else very near, he muttered, 'I still think this is an infatuation.'

Tessa put the glass to her lips. 'No,' she said gently, 'you were the infatuation.'

Paul had been the shadow, Orme was the substance. She looked across at Orme, and Paul knew that the comparison had to go against himself. He said bitterly, 'Oh yes, he's got presence, he's a very physical man,' and Tessa laughed.

'Not the sort you'd push if you had any sense,' she said, keeping her voice and her laughter down. 'But within that rugged physique is an alarmingly high I.Q.'

'How do you expect to live up to such a paragon?' Paul sneered, and a wave of loneliness almost engulfed her at the thought of life without Orme.

She said coldly, to quieten Paul, 'Five years ago no one thought I could live up to you, and I don't think Orme wants to be lived up to, just lived with.'

That was dreaming again. Dangerous dreaming. She remembered Orme laughing at himself, at what he said others would be saying, 'Not an easy man to live with.' Not easy, no, but a marvellous man to live with, a man whom it would be bitterly hard to live without.

With a word of apology to the little group of whom he had been the centre Orme came across to her. It had looked rather as though she and Paul were chatting confidentially. Everyone here but the team knew how things had been in the old days between those two, and by now the team, trained observers in sizing up a situation, probably had their own ideas.

When Orme strode with an air of purpose straight for Tessa it was plain he was going to break up that tête-à-tête, and the second hush of the evening settled on the room.

Reaching Tessa, he lifted his hand and touched her cheek gently, then he took her hand and drew her towards him, away from Paul. The gesture was intimate and at the same time a public avowal, and Paul said jerkily, 'Tessa tells me you're a judo black belt.'

He had to say something. He fancied himself as the artistic type, although he had never created anything in his life. He would have liked to call this powerfully built man a thug, but he was not risking open insult. He stopped at insolence, 'A judo black belt' shuddering fastidiously as though that made Orme a bullying oaf. He sounded, Tessa decided, amused, almost exactly like his mother might have done.

'Did she now?' Orme spoke softly, smiling. 'I wonder why she decided to mention that?'

He had been unfailingly amiable since they arrived, no guest could have been more charming, but now, suddenly, there was a cold and controlled menace in him, more frightening than any amount of ranting and raving would have been.

He was telling Paul, telling all of them, that Tessa had told him the whole story, and Paul must presume on nothing. Not on Tessa retaining any scrap of her one-time feelings for him, and least of all on Orme allowing him to make a nuisance of himself. Any move from you to take Tessa away from me, said Orme, without needing words, and in the most civilised manner I will hammer you straight into the ground.

Paul Mellor knew he was looking at a dangerous man, whose wealth and power completely outstripped his own. Orme took Tessa with him, and this time Paul did not follow.

'You missed your chance there,' one of the men said to Paul, as Tessa stood with Orme, the stars of the show, smiling, talking, a vibrantly exciting woman. 'Not that I blame you,' said Paul Mellor's friend. 'None of us had any idea she was going to turn out like this.'

He sighed at his own lack of foresight. Little Tessa Harris, remembered as 'that kid who had the crush on Paul Mellor', had developed into a woman who would have been an ideal wife for a junior executive on a company ladder, like himself.

He wasn't the only man tonight finding Tessa attractive. They all did, but not of them was chancing his luck with Orme Jared there. The way Jared had just dealt with Paul was warning enough.

Tessa got enough invitations to have filled all the evenings she had left in this town, but each time the invitation included Orme. She couldn't have imagined a more triumphant return to the little group that had almost hounded her out of Blackstone. When she said, 'It's been a lovely party,' it really had been, and she was quite sorry for Paul, who looked so sad as he said goodnight.

This time Paul didn't hold her hand. Nor would he be calling in the Stag's Head tomorrow on the offchance of finding her there, because there was an offchance of finding Orme too. Paul had been well and truly scared off.

As the team walked towards their cars Annie whispered behind her hand to Tessa, 'He's good-looking all right, but I should stick with Orme if I were you.'

That was a laugh and Annie meant it to be. Any woman would 'stick with Orme'. Against Orme Paul Mellor was a poor fish.

The inn was in darkness, except for an occasional guiding light. Orme had the key to the back door and they trooped in silently, going quietly up the stairs to their bedrooms. On the top landing Orme said 'Goodnight.'

'Goodnight.' With her hand on the doorknob Tessa asked, 'Will you come to the houses we were asked to?'

'Of course.'

He reached his door, opened it and went in, closing the door, and Tessa stepped into her own dark bedroom. She reached for the wall switch, filling the room with light, but it was still an empty room.

A goodnight kiss would have made her less lonely. Even a passing touch on the shoulder as he went would have been something to take to bed with her. His arm had been around her tonight so no one should think she was available, but after he had scared them off there had been nothing to say but 'Goodnight', and close your door quietly.

He needed her, part of the team; but she loved him. If it was love. There was certainly physical attraction, sharp and sweet, filling her with a sensuous longing.

She crossed to the dividing door between the two

rooms, placing her fingertips against it as though she might tap softly. If she did Orme would open the door and her hands would touch the velvet of his coat, slide round his neck.

'I was a hit tonight, wasn't I?' she would say. 'Hardly a man there who wouldn't have enjoyed kissing me goodnight, so why don't you?'

If she did that Orme would kiss her and she would go up in flames. If she invited him to make love to her of course he would, and of course she wouldn't. She wanted him, as she had never wanted anyone or anything, but she couldn't have survived a casual affair.

She stepped back from the dividing door, her hands falling limply to her sides. She loved him. She wanted to grow old with him. She was alone in her room and she felt as though she was alone in the world.

The filming proceeded with the usual hitches; and with the Orme Jared panache the story of the Grey Lady pit and the men who had worked it took shape.

Characters, long gone, lived again: a poet of robust dialect verse, a near-saint who had preached at the coal face, footballers, cricketers, rogues, eccentrics.

The coalmine itself was the centrepiece, but filming there had to be limited. There was no longer any way down to the subterranean workings. The cage machinery had rusted and landfalls had blocked the air shafts. But the filming they did around the ruins of the mine had a stark haunting quality that satisfied everybody.

Days were full. Evenings too. The team had a social life in Blackstone for as long as they wanted it. Nothing very glamorous or exciting, but open doors and a host of would-be hosts and hostesses. Tessa and Orme went to several dinner parties and if Orme was bored he didn't show it.

Tessa counted off the days with dread. Soon the closeness would be over. She would never almost—share a room with Orme again. It would never again be 'Orme and Tessa'. As soon as they left here the rot would have to set in so that this hollow 'engagement' could collapse.

The team would be sorry. They had all taken to the idea, especially Annie, who took it for granted that Tessa would be moving into Orme's home—and Spike's and Annie's—right away.

'No,' said Tessa.

'No?' echoed Annie. 'Well, the place is big enough for you to have your own bedroom if that's what you want. Anyhow, when are you getting married?'

'There's no hurry,' said Tessa. 'No rush.'

But their stay in Blackstone came to an end and Mr and Mrs Mann, proprietors of the Stag's Head, were sorry to be losing the team. They had brought in the customers. On the last evening there would be customers coming in to say goodbye.

Tessa thought that Paul might turn up. She had seen him once or twice in other people's houses, and she suspected he would turn up tonight and say something like, 'I'm here if ever you need me.' Paul Mellor would be no man to saddle with your troubles, but she felt it was the kind of thing he might say.

She never knew if Paul did come to the Stag's Head that last evening, because she wasn't there herself. During the afternoon Orme said, 'Shall we eat out tonight?'

'I'd like that,' she said promptly, hoping he meant the two of them, not the whole team. They had been almost inseparable these three weeks, but only alone at night, up on that top floor, in their separate beds in their separate rooms.

It seemed that Orme did mean just the two of them for dinner, although he probably wanted her reassurance that she was staying with the team, and to discuss how they were going to break off their engagement.

She took care dressing. Every evening since they came here she had taken care, making herself as good to look at as she possibly could.

Professionally she and Orme had everything in common. She talked his language as far as the job went, if he would only see her as an attractive woman too. He was never going to pay her closer attention than now, so every evening she had used every scrap of her skill. If Orme didn't appreciate it others did. Everyone thought she looked wonderful. 'It suits you,' said Spike.

'What suits me?'

He grinned knowingly. Falling in love, he meant, being loved; and he was half way right.

Tonight she came downstairs with her fur coat over her long red velvet skirt and a high-necked black silky sweater, a wide black velvet band holding her hair back from her face.

'Where are we going?' she asked, settling comfortably in the car, and Orme said,

'I thought we might try the famous Goat at Elmbridge.'

That was where Paul had taken her in the old days. It wasn't famous, Orme knew it wasn't, but it had been a good eating place and they said it was still. 'Is that all right?' He was asking her a serious question. If she had said,

'I'd rather somewhere else,' somewhere else they would have gone, but of course it didn't matter.

'Fine,' she said. 'It's under new management, but they used to do a super duck à l'orange.'

'That sounds all right,' said Orme. She didn't have to tell him the way, he must have asked someone the directions. He drove straight there.

The last time Tessa had walked into this glowing place—it was mellowly lit, the tables in alcoves under little yellow lamps—she had been Paul Mellor's adoring slave. Such a child she had been. She was a woman now, a strong woman with a stronger man who would have no time at all for an adoring slave. But he would have been kinder to that girl than Paul had been. She hoped he would be kinder to the woman, although she had more sense now than to wear her heart on her sleeve.

'Has it changed?' Orme asked her.

They had food in front of them—the duck, having praised it she felt she had better ask for it—and red wine in tall tulip glasses.

'No.' Perhaps it had, here and there. The seating was the same, so was the lighting, and probably the menu. She wasn't sure she could remember it that clearly, nor even Paul sitting opposite her. She looked around, 'I don't think it has,' and then back at Orme, and he blotted out Paul's memory completely.

He knew she had thought of Paul. He said quietly, 'Has Mellor been in touch with you again?'

It wouldn't have been easy, without Orme knowing, but it might have been managed if Paul had been made of sterner stuff. 'You scared him off,' she said.

153

His eyes scanned her face and there was a tug of a smile on her lips and his smile widened to a grin. 'You wouldn't want a man who was scared of me, would you?'

'No.' She laughed openly. 'But it does shorten the list.' And while they were laughing she asked what she wanted to know. 'Does Anthea Vella know about this?' 'This' was the ring, and Orme said,

'We were at the parting of the ways.'

That was the best of news. That took the laughter deep inside her. 'Like Derek and me,' she said. 'He phoned here and Annie told him I was engaged to you.'

'Does that surprise him?' Orme didn't say Annie had been spreading a false report, and Tessa said gaily,

'Seems not. He said I was always talking about work anyway.' She took a sip of her wine, and shrugged, 'So the job wins again.'

'Does it?' asked Orme.

'I think so.' She knew so. Not only for the job's sake, but because she could not go away from him.

'After you leave here shall you keep in touch?'

He wanted to be sure Paul could not pull her back. She answered sensibly. Telling him that no man could take her from him would be more reassurance than he wanted. You shouldn't offer anyone more than they wanted if rejection would tear you apart.

She said, light and easy, 'You mean what happens when I'm no longer supposed to be engaged to you?' Even if she told no one in Blackstone the end of Orme Jared's engagement to the girl in his team would probably get a paragraph in the press. If it had been wider known that Tessa was wearing his ring some gossip columnist would have been on to them by now. 'Then Paul will very likely get in touch with me,' said Tessa. 'But then I'll be a long way away.'

She was as far away from Paul as she was from the moon, there was no contact at all. But as she sat facing Orme she felt as though her hands would reach out on their own, without her brain telling them to, her hair would curl towards him like the tendrils of a clinging plant.

She said, a little breathlessly, 'What do we do about this?' The ring again.

'Leave it for a week or so,' said Orme

She had another week or two. It didn't mean much, they had to taper off the understanding, hadn't they? But it meant a little more time to make Orme decide he liked being with her, alone with her.

Her eyes held his. 'All right,' she said. Make love to me, said her eyes. Say something that will give me an opening in the armour of your self-control.

He didn't make love to her, instead he made her laugh. They had a lovely evening, talking about many things. They discussed, argued, talked, and Orme made her laugh. When they got up to leave most of the tables had already emptied.

They were bowed to the door and urged to come again, and Tessa thought—they'll remember us. They'll remember Orme, the kind of customer any restaurant would welcome.

She would remember this evening too, clearer than any evening out with Paul.

Paul had never made her laugh at all. And Paul, as every hour in Orme's company was increasingly proving to her, she had never loved.

CHAPTER EIGHT

'Are you in a hurry to get home tomorrow?' Orme had asked Tessa as they drove back to the Stag's Head.

'No hurry at all,' she'd said.

'Shall we call in at Midwinton?'

'I'd like that very much.'

The detour could be done and still get them to London by evening. She didn't ask if Spike and Annie would be coming too. If he'd said 'Yes' her joy would have been diminished, so she didn't risk it, and that meant she fell asleep happy and woke hoping for a lovely day.

Her case was packed and this was goodbye to the room with the dividing door that had stayed shut. Maybe she could knock on it this morning, just to see it open and Orme standing there. But she couldn't. Not even in broad daylight.

She fastened her case, did a final check of drawers and wardrobe, and stepped out into the corridor, loaded with case, coat, boots and salad bowl.

Orme's door was open; he'd gone down ahead of her, so if she had tapped on the dividing door it would have made no difference. But *please* let it be just the two of them going to Midwinton.

By the time she got downstairs it had all been arranged. Spike and Annie were travelling back in the van. Today was Thursday, the team would meet again in the office on Monday, and everyone presumed that Orme and Tessa were off to Lady Ursula's house for the weekend. Tessa left that unqueried too. She had nothing to get back to the flat for. She could stay till Sunday if she was invited.

Saying goodbye, Annie whispered, 'It's the most gorgeous place, you're going to love it.' Spike and Annie had been to Midwinton, but this would be Tessa's first visit, and she would be going as Orme's fiancée. Lady Ursula believed that, and this visit would reinforce the deception, so Orme couldn't be wanting too quick a return of the ring that Tessa wore. The original reason for her wearing it was over. If Orme put off taking it back he must have his own reason for wanting her to go on wearing it.

Snow had been falling from early morning, light feathery flakes. It snowed all the way, not heavily but persistent enough to keep the windscreen wipers going and the roads hazardous. By the time they reached the Cotswolds a silent whiteness had settled on hills and houses.

Tessa recalled her own return to Blackstone. Orme was coming now to the place where he was born, but that was where the similarity ended. Although as he told her the names of the places they were passing, and something about most of them, she was reminded of herself describing the surroundings of Blackstone to him. A gulf divides us, she thought, and at the same time—nothing need divide us, we could be so close.

The village of Midwinton was built partly on a hillside, where cottages clustered above the winding main road. The church and the village green were white under the falling snow, and just beyond the church stood the lodge and the entrance to the hall.

The gates were open. As they drove through a woman came out and Orme tooted the horn in greeting. Tessa, turning, saw her wave and step back into the lodge out of the snow.

There had once been a curving avenue of magnificent elms here, but now there were spindly saplings where some of the elms had stood. Orme said, 'We're planting beeches, and still hoping to save the elms that are left.'

He was talking of the elm plague that had ravaged the countryside. It would be a long time before the new trees were as splendid as the old, but Lady Ursula's great-grandchildren might see them towering against the skyline. These trees had been planted for the future.

And then the car rounded the curve of the drive, and there was the house, and Tessa gave a soft gasp of pleasure. She had been prepared for a splendid house, but not for this enchantment.

It wasn't large for a manor house. It was two-storeyed unless you counted the dormer windows in the snow-covered roof, in Cotswold stone and as right in its setting as the trees; as though like them it had grown and had deep roots.

A hill rose behind it, with a little folly of a summer house that you would reach by climbing a winding path. At the side of the house was a small frozen lake, and lights glowed in the mullioned windows although it was still afternoon.

It was the kind of house that could cast a spell over you. The photograph she had seen had been dull and flat compared with the reality. This house was warm and living, and she said, 'It—is— beautiful,' pausing between the words because they sounded inadequate.

She knew now why Orme had said there would never be anywhere like Midwinton for him. Once this had been your home it would always be in your heart. His London house was lovely, but this was a house you would love.

He stopped the car near the flight of three shallow steps that led to the main door and said, 'We're home.'

He was home. Tessa was only a guest here, but if she had said that she would have spoiled this wonderful feeling that was like a homecoming.

'Do you have to get to London tonight?' he asked.

'No.'

'You'll stay for the weekend?'

'I'd like to.'

'Good,' he said.

She stepped out of that car feeling as though she had come to the end of a long journey and here was home. Perhaps it was the charm of the house. Perhaps it was the man with her, who had asked her to stay ... You are my home, my country, my world ...

He could be too. She wanted him more than any other man in the world, but she mustn't let her hopes run so far ahead. She hungered for him, but she might have to live without him, except as a business colleague. He could be fostering this empathy between them just to keep her happy in her career. Could he? *Could* he? He had said he would do anything to keep her in the team, but surely not this?

The door opened as they reached it and two red setters hurtled out at Orme, their long feathery tails swishing a wild and joyous welcome. He spoke to them, and patted them, and they quietened, keeping close bèside him, tails still wagging, as he and Tessa walked into the house.

The man who had opened the door was tall, stooping slightly, with a long jaw and a high forehead from which the hair had almost totally receded. When he wasn't smiling he probably looked mournful, but he was smiling broadly now.

'Hello, Jenkins,' said Orme.

'Good to see you, sir,' said the man. 'And Miss Harris.'

He knew Tessa's name, and from the way he was beaming on them both he knew she was supposed to be marrying Orme.

Lady Ursula was standing in the doorway, in an archway with a pointed top that made an attractive frame for her. Leaning on her ebony cane, in a black velvet dress or housecoat, with long sweeping sleeves and skirt, she was so regal that Tessa wondered wildly if she was supposed to bob down in a curtsey.

'I was just beginning to be concerned about you,' Lady Ursula said in her beautifully modulated voice. 'But now that you are safely here I hope that the snow gets thicker. It would be delightful if we could all be snowed in together for a few days.'

Orme laughed. 'Sorry, grandmamma, but Tessa and I are out of here on Monday if I have to dig a tunnel.' He kissed her, and she was obviously waiting for Tessa to kiss her too. As Tessa's lips touched the old lady's cheek Lady Ursula put an arm around the girl and drew her close in a warm and loving embrace.

Unexpected tears filled Tessa's eyes. It was a long, long time since she had known anything as near as this to mother-love.

'Come to the fire,' said Orme's grandmother, holding Tessa, taking her into a little parlour, which was really a fair sized room but seemed small after the galleried height of the entrance hall, and had all the signs of being a favourite living room.

It was elegant with Georgian bureaux, corner cupboard and tables; but cosy with curtains, Victorian chesterfield and chairs, covered in matching cabbage-rose chintz. Sofas and several chairs were grouped around the hearth, where a coal fire was burning. On a small table, beside an upright chair, was a tapestry frame, the needle stabbed into the tapestry and coloured wools filling a basket.

Lady Ursula took the upright chair, and Orme guided Tessa to an armchair nearer the fire. She sank down into it so far that she had a little un-dignified struggle to get herself upright again. You could fall asleep in these down cushions, but not under Lady Ursula's eyes—Tessa was far from feeling that relaxed. She edged herself forward and sat with her feet on the ground.

Orme smiled at her, putting another cushion be-hind her that propped her up, telling her, 'I tend to forget how tiny you are.'

'So do I,' she said, 'until I lean back in big chairs.'

There were smaller, neater chairs around and next time she would watch that she got one. If there was a next time. There was this weekend, but after that she didn't know.

'You must be ready for a cup of tea,' said Orme's grandmother, and right on cue Miss Burton backed into the room carrying a loaded tray which Orme took from her.

Miss Burton was his grandmother's companion, brisk and hearty and as pleased to see them as every-one else in this house seemed to be. The dogs lay at Orme's feet, their tails still swishing in rhythmic unison, and Lady Ursula sat in her high-backed chair, looking like a queen with her favourites.

No, that wasn't right. She was a woman with her family. Alice would look just as proud and con-tented, when she had her children and grand-children around her table. Like Alice, Lady Ursula had photographs on the mantelpiece, on the desk, on the walls.

Miss Burton poured tea and offered sandwiches, and Orme's grandmother saw where Tessa was looking and said, 'That is my husband.' There were two photographs in matching silver frames on the desk: a young sailor and an old man, ruggedly handsome; Lt. William Orme Jared and Admiral Jared, R.N. retired. Orme had the same look, and Tessa said,

'May I?' and scrambled to her feet and went closer.

'Don't start on them,' said Orme, 'or you'll be here for hours. I want to show you round the house before it gets dark.'

It was still snowing outside, the white sky was dulling with the approach of night.

Tessa went back to her seat. This room, she felt, was a female retreat. Generations of women had probably sat in here, sewing and gossiping and sipping tea.

The teacups were in such exquisite eggshell china that she was almost scared to hold them. They looked odd in Orme's strong hands, but he was used to them, they wouldn't scare him as they did Tessa. She was relieved when she reached the bottom of her cup and could put it down and say, 'No more, thank you.'

As she did Orme stood up, and so did the dogs. 'Come on,' he said, and while his grandmother was protesting that Tessa could see around the house tomorrow he led the way back into the entrance hall, dogs at his heels, closing the parlour door as soon as Tessa stepped through.

The entrance was a magnificent room, the polished floor covered with dark red Persian carpets, the walls pale green, the doors white. Some doors were set in pointed arches, the double doors to the main rooms were flanked with white pillars and topped by a deep carved archway. The gallery, at the top of the stairs, was in shadow until Orme switched on the huge bronze chandelier high above and then Tessa glimpsed other doors and archways.

She felt a rising surge of excitement. She wanted to walk through every door, to see everything; and Orme showed her round as though her pleasure in it all pleased him.

She could understand why it meant so much to him. It was a delightful house. She saw the splendid rooms that were only occasionally used, and the lovely rooms that were lived in. She walked the long gallery, looking at the portraits; and she stood in a room at the top of the house that had once been a schoolroom.

It was plainly furnished, with a large central table, and before Eton and Oxford this was where Orme's education had begun. A dividing door led into the nursery, and Tessa clasped her hands together as she stepped in there, because these toys would have captivated anyone who was young at heart.

She could have played for hours with the five-foot-high Victorian dolls' house, and as for the rocking horse—who was black as jet, with flaring nostrils and glaring eyes, and long silky black mane and tail—she would rather have taken him home with her than almost anything else in the house. Except Orme, of course. She smiled at the thought, and stroked the silky mane and set the horse rocking.

There was no dust. You would have expected an unused feel in here, but it didn't seem like a room that was shut up. Model railway lines ran over there, by the big housekeeper's cupboard, and surely they weren't old. They looked almost new. Orme said, as she frowned, puzzled, 'Children still play in here. Friends' and relations' children.'

Relations were family, and there were photographs of children downstairs in the small parlour. 'Won't your grandmother settle for them?' Tessa asked.

'She may have to,' said Orme cheerfully. 'She doesn't always get her own way.'

The horse rocked on as they left the room. 'I'm glad children still play with him,' said Tessa. 'I'd hate to think of him shut away on his own.'

Night had fallen and all the lights were on when her tour of the house ended and she stood with Orme, on the gallery, at the door of the room which would be hers for the weekend. 'I wonder you can bear to leave this place,' she said.

'I couldn't lead the life of a country squire,' he said. 'Not for another thirty years. But I need it to come back to.'

It seemed that the men in this family often had other jobs. There was a bewigged high court judge in the long gallery, and a sprinkling of army and navy. Orme's father had been a surgeon. 'Who runs things?' Tessa asked, and Orme smiled.

'My grandmother is still very much the chatelaine.'

Of course she was, thought Tessa. Ursula Jared would have made a successful business woman in the outside world. They wouldn't have retired her from the board of directors without a struggle.

'Jack Duncan, who manages the estate, will probably be along tonight,' said Orme.

That was someone else Tessa would be meeting in her supposed role as the future Mrs Orme Jared, but if it didn't worry Orme it didn't worry her, and when Jack Duncan did arrive, after dinner, she enjoyed his appreciative reaction when he was introduced to her. Men often eyed her admiringly, but this man was considering her as Orme's wife, and he thought she was right, and that gave her confidence a boost.

Orme went off with Jack Duncan, and Lady Ursula, who was busy with her tapestry, immediately directed a look at Miss Burton that said, 'Kindly leave us alone.'

Up jumped Miss Burton, muttering about making a phone call, and Tessa watched her go, then waited to hear what Lady Ursula had to say to her that needed privacy. She might have guessed.

'Now,' said Lady Ursula, needle suspended, bright blue eyes needle-sharp, 'tell me. When is this wedding?'

Tessa floundered, and gulped, 'You'd—better ask Orme.'

'Orme won't tell me.' His grandmother glared at Tessa as though this was a conspiracy of silence against herself, and Tessa swallowed again and licked at dry lips.

What could she say? If she tried excuses like, 'We haven't set a date,' Lady Ursula would be setting one for them. What would Orme want her to say? She said, 'It's only a week or so since we got engaged, and an engagement has to last long enough for you to be quite sure, doesn't it? That's what an engagement is about, isn't it?'

Not in Lady Ursula's book, going by the uncompromising set of her mouth. An engagement was a promise, and promises were never broken, and she went on glaring at Tessa, who could only say wretchedly, 'I'm sorry, but I just don't know.'

The old woman and the girl looked straight at

each other, and slowly the glare in the blue eyes subsided. The still-dark head bowed again over the tapestry and another minute repairing stitch was made. When Lady Ursula looked up again she was almost smiling. She said, 'Well, I see I must be content to know that he is getting married, and that Orme's children will live here even if I'm not around to see them.'

Playing in the nursery, running through the rooms, for a little while learning lessons around the schoolroom table. 'His sons,' murmured Tessa, and Lady Ursula said, quite indignantly,

'A daughter would be as welcome as a son.'

'Oh!' Tessa had taken it for granted that Lady Ursula hankered for great-grandsons. It might never be Tessa's concern, but she said, as though it was, 'I'm glad to hear that. I always thought the story of Catherine of Aragon was one of the saddest in history.'

Suddenly the atmosphere was cosy again. Lady Ursula stitched away, and Tessa relaxed into the corner of the chesterfield. The fire crackled and the clocked ticked and Lady Ursula said, 'I was almost giving up hope that Orme would ever find the right girl.'

Tessa hoped that he had with all her heart.

The needle went slowly in and out. A flower had frayed on a cushion cover and the petal was growing again in the same faded colours. Lady Ursula gave a throaty little chuckle. 'Yes, I did. I nearly gave up hope. Do you know, I was always threatening to disinherit him if he didn't find me a nice granddaughter.'

Tessa laughed too, while her shining world collapsed.

That would explain everything. Orme needed a

fiancée. Not necessarily to marry, but to show to his grandmother if he wanted to keep Midwinton. And he did. He wanted this house.

Perhaps he reasoned that Lady Ursula had only a little longer to live and it would make her happy to believe he would be marrying some time. It was making her happy. It was also making sure that she didn't leave Midwinton to one of Orme's second cousins or whoever the other relations were, who already had children who came here and played here.

In the first place Tessa was almost sure he had entered into this masquerade to keep her away from Paul and in the team. Professionally it had worked well. Perhaps this was a personal bonus he hadn't expected, but he should have told her why he wanted her to come here today still wearing that ring, pretending to everyone that they loved each other.

She *did* love him, that was the hell of it. If he had told her why he wanted to go on with this farce she just might have agreed. One good turn deserved another. He had freed her of Paul, supported her through the weeks at Blackstone, so why shouldn't she help him keep this house where he was born?

She didn't believe Lady Ursula would leave it to anyone but Orme, but she didn't know for sure. She didn't know Lady Ursula. She didn't know Orme. She didn't know anybody, except herself, and she knew for sure what a fool she could be.

Lady Ursula went on talking, about the photographs around them, and Tessa looked interested and made quite sensible remarks, her mind functioning on two levels.

Miss Burton peered in and then came in; obviously there was no longer anything confidential going on here. She took her chair by the fire, making up a cosy little threesome, and Tessa heard herself telling them about work, laughing at jokes. She heard the other two women, and all the time, inside her, she was cold and sad and alone.

When Orme came back with the estate manager she turned a bright smile on both men, and Jack Duncan shook hands with her, saying it had been great meeting her and he and his wife would be seeing a lot more of her, wouldn't they? Tessa went on smiling. 'It's been lovely meeting you,' she said. 'Goodnight.'

She was still sitting on the chesterfield and Orme sat down beside her, his arm on the back of the sofa behind her. When he touched her she moved away a little, and she knew he noticed because he took his arm away, but she couldn't help it. She was sick of the pretence because she had begun to hope they weren't pretending. She had thought he touched her because he wanted to, and she still wanted to be touched, and that was what frightened her.

Lady Ursula went to bed early, and Miss Burton kept the same hours. 'Early to bed, early to rise,' quoted Miss Burton as the clock began to chime. Before it finished chiming Lady Ursula had grasped her cane, and Miss Burton was offering her a supporting arm.

'Yes indeed,' said Tessa. She had the beginning of a nervous headache, taut at the back of the neck, tightening her forehead, and a dark room and a cool pillow might stave it off. She might not sleep, but once she was in her bedroom she could stop acting as though she hadn't a care in the world.

But Orme didn't let her go. As she leaned forward he stood up, standing before her. She would have moved into his arms, or at the very least very

168

close to him, so she stayed where she was for the moment.

Lady Ursula and Miss Burton said goodnight. Orme opened the door for them, saw them out into the hall, and then turned back to ask Tessa, 'Do you want a drink?'

'No, thank you.'

It was ridiculously early for bed by their standards, but she didn't want to sit here talking, not even about impersonal things. He walked across to the fireplace and stood there. The dogs, who had trotted to the door with him, stretched out on the rug at his feet, and Tessa said, 'Do they always follow you everywhere when you're here?'

'Most of the time.' He glanced down at the animals, then up at the girl, looking at her steadily. 'What's the matter?' he asked.

'Nothing,' she said, instinctively and too fast, and then as he waited and she knew that she would have to answer, 'Except that I feel more of a fraud here than I did at Blackstone.' She was twisting her ring on her finger. 'There was no one there who this was going to hurt,' she said, 'but here there is.'

'Yes.' His grandmother would take the return of her ring badly. Tessa knew how badly, she knew what was at stake. 'How does it feel to you?' Orme asked.

'What?'

'Would you consider wearing it a little longer?'

'Why?' He might tell her now what was at stake. If he did she supposed she would agree.

'At the same time,' he said quietly, 'you might consider marrying me.'

She wasn't sure she had heard that right. 'I might——?' Her voice rose. 'Marrying *you*?' It went up into a squeak again, then it came flat and tone-

169

less. 'To please your grandmother?'

'I was thinking more of pleasing you and myself,' said Orme drily. His eyes were still steady and calm. He looked attractive, charming; as always—successful and in charge. He did not look like a man asking a woman to marry him. He said, 'I think I could please you,' and in spite of everything shivers ran down her spine, little frissons of delight.

If Orme made love to her it would be everything her body would ever want, but would that be enough? There wasn't much trust being shown, he wasn't trusting her with the reason why. Of course he could please a woman, he was experienced and accomplished, but he was not offering love in any sense but the sensual.

'Oh yes,' she said, 'but marriage is a long-term contract, isn't it?'

There would have to be more than sex to make a true marriage, especially in these days when marriages shattered so easily. Look at Paul and Stella. Look at so many people. 'Or would ours have a get-out clause?' she asked, and her voice was clear and cool. 'Would we try for a while and promise to part without a fuss when either of us wanted our freedom back?'

'I couldn't promise you that,' he said.

He could not have been more controlled if they had been talking shop. She had seen him looking a great deal more involved and animated at work. He hadn't even come to sit beside her. He was standing there by the fireplace, the dogs at his feet, asking her to consider marrying him. No hurry, of course, so long as she went on wearing Lady Ursula's ring and everyone went on believing a marriage was imminent.

She asked, 'Why do you want to marry me?' Because it's time you married someone and I fit the bill? Because we're in the same line of business and your grandmother seems to like me and maybe she wasn't joking about this house? 'What kind of wife do you think I'd make?' she demanded, sitting ramrod straight, tension throbbing in her temples.

'The kind I want,' he said. 'I think we should have a good marriage.'

'A marriage to our mutual advantage?'

He got Midwinton and she got him. She could see the advantage in that. She got Orme, and she wanted him as much as he wanted Midwinton. 'You could say that,' he said.

If he had shown any emotion deeper than this friendly suggestion that they might suit each other well enough, then she would have said '*Yes*,' but this chilled her blood. And it angered her, because he should have told her why. Either that or pretend he loved her. One thing or the other.

'What would it involve?' She could be cool. She might even hurt him a little, or at least shake him by facing facts.

'What does marriage usually involve?' he said quietly, and her cheeks warmed although her blood was chilled. She said, as though she was talking shop too,

'I mean, how soon would your grandmother be expecting those great-grandchildren? Would you divorce me if I turned out to be barren? Two women in every ten are, I believe, so it's always a possibility, and I would like to know what would be expected of me.'

'I am not in the market for a brood mare,' he said coldly, as though this was beginning to bore him. 'I'm asking you to wear the ring a little longer, and if you find you're getting used to it I should be honoured and delighted to discuss how we might proceed from there.'

She couldn't look at him, but she muttered, 'All right,' and rubbed her forehead, along the hairline, and explained, 'I've got a bit of a headache.'

The last time she had used that excuse had been at Blackstone, during that evening conference when her mind had been in a whirl over Paul. She had wanted to get away from Orme then, and she did now, and he remembered.

She started to chatter. 'I think I'll go to my room—I've rather a lot to think about. It isn't every day someone asks me to marry him. That was a marriage proposal, wasn't it? Or was it a proposal that I should go on wearing your grandmother's ring to keep your grandmother happy?'

'You talk too much,' said Orme wearily.

'So you tell me.'

He came and sat beside her, taking her into his arms. It was done without fuss, so naturally that she put up no resistance. She thought dully—does he know I could never fight him, that all he has to do is open his arms to me? He said, 'I shouldn't like you to go to bed with a headache,' and drew her head down against his shoulder, gently massaging the back of her neck.

At first even the light touch of fingertips was painful, but almost at once she was relaxing. If he gave her nothing else he gave her physical comfort. She could close her eyes and listen to the sound of his heart beating, and feel the pain ebbing away under a firmer fingertip pressure.

This wasn't imagination. This really was taking her headache away. He turned her head so that she faced him, but she still kept her eyes shut while his firm and gentle touch, on her temples and along the hairline of her forehead, was lifting the pounding tension of the pain.

When she smiled he said, 'Better?'

'Mmm, yes.' She opened her eyes and she was sitting back, no longer supported. She said, half smiling, 'Paul said you were a very physical man.'

'Did he?' Both eyebrows rose. 'And what did he mean by that? That I was likely to be a clumsy lover or an impatient one?'

She knew what Paul had meant. He had resented Orme's powerful personality, that everyone at that party thought Orme Jared a more impressive man than Paul Mellor. She said very slowly, 'I didn't ask. I'm sure you're not clumsy. I always thought you were impatient, but that was at work.'

'I can be patient,' said Orme.

She was sure he could. He could play a waiting game if that was the winning way. He sat there now, beside her, as self-contained as though they were both in the office, and this time she did scramble to her feet, and blurted, 'I want to go to bed.'

He stood up too, and drawled, 'Alone, of course,' as if she had thought he might suggest accompanying her. She thought he was laughing at her.

'Goodnight,' she said.

'Goodnight.' He opened the door for her, and she crossed the hall and climbed the curving staircase. It seemed to take a long time before she reached the top to walk along the gallery, where she could glance down into the hall without obviously looking back.

There was no one down there. He hadn't watched her. He had gone back into the room and closed the door.

Lights were on in her room, and it was a beautiful room.

The bed, a brass fourposter, was covered with a white lace bedspread, with pink bed draperies matching a deep pink frieze on the white walls. It was a big bed, much too big for one, turned down, her nightdress lying waiting for her; and she sank down on to it, her head in her hands, trying to understand just what had been happening downstairs just now.

The more she thought about that marriage proposal the less likely it seemed, but it could have been genuine. Orme had said she was the kind of wife he wanted, that a marriage could be to their mutual advantage. That could be true enough, Orme was no hypocrite; he had never once said, 'I love you.'

CHAPTER NINE

THE first thing that came into Tessa's mind next morning, even before she opened her eyes, was last night's conversation with Orme. She woke calmer than she had fallen asleep, but unable to relax again into slumber and unwilling to lie here, waiting for that cup of tea she had been told would arrive at eight o'clock.

She showered in the little pink bathroom that led off her bedroom, and came back to start dressing. She *was* calm this morning. It was a calming scene outside, serene, snow-covered and silent, and she had decided that the best thing she could do would be to take this weekend hour by hour, and try not to spoil it. One way or another the future would happen, but these three days were surely going to be happy.

She had never stayed in a lovelier house, nor slept in a more attractive guestroom. She wondered who had been here before her. Probably most of Orme's other ladies, and she wondered if they had slept alone and her resolution to stay cool went up in smoke. She burned with jealousy, furious with herself but shaking with it, so that she had to turn her back on the room and walk to the window and look out again at the still white world.

If she and Orme ever did marry she couldn't bear it if there were other women. She didn't think there would be, she couldn't see Orme cheating his wife, but what was more likely was that Tessa would never be his wife. Some time the 'engagement' would peter out, and if she was still with the team she would know who he was escorting. People would talk, the woman would phone him at work. She wasn't sure she could stand that either. She was almost absolutely certain that she could not. There might be a tough future waiting, but not today.

She made herself walk steadily to the door, breathing slowly and practising a happy expression, so that she smiled easily when she met the girl who would have brought up her tea in another half hour, and who said, 'You're down early, miss.'

'Sorry,' said Tessa. 'Is no one else around?' What about Miss Burton's early-to-bed-early-to-rise?

'Mr Orme is,' said the girl. 'He's in the study.'

Tessa knew the way. She tapped on the door and Orme was sitting behind a big carved black oak desk, very unlike the stark steel and leather modern desk he used in the office. But the same man, dealing with papers in front of him.

'Sorry,' she said again. 'Am I interrupting?'

'I'd hope to finish before you were down. I won't be long. Have you had breakfast?'

'No, but I'm all right.' He knew she wasn't much of a breakfast eater.

He had a pot of coffee on the desk beside him and he said, 'There's plenty of this and it's still hot. Ring for another cup.'

'I'll fetch one,' she said. She sat on a chair by the window, drinking her coffee, while Orme went on with his paperwork. As he initialled the last sheet he said,

'Now I'll show you around outside.'

It had stopped snowing, but it was still freezing hard and the air was so sharp it caught your breath. They walked to the stables and Tessa fed a magnificent pure-bred Arab horse an apple. 'Do you ride?' Orme asked her.

'No.' The horse seemed as tall as a house, and Orme smiled.

'This isn't the weather to start learning.'

The ground was like iron, the lake was frozen solid, the ducks appeared to be skating on it; and when they climbed the hill to the little Victorian temple-folly of a summerhouse Tessa slid back about one step in three. Orme must have been wearing boots with more grip in the soles because most of the time he was hauling her up.

They laughed a lot, and the view was worth the climb when you reached the summerhouse. The gardens and the village were spread out for you. 'It's a beautiful view,' she said.

'That it is.' He smiled at her and as she laughed back she thought—he's being the perfect host, but he isn't giving any more of himself than a good host would.

There was no talk of marriage today. Last night had given her no power over him. She could make him smile, she knew she could make him angry, but nothing she could do or say could make him vulnerable, and she felt that he would dislike to discover how vulnerable she was.

'I feel such a fool,' she had said at the beginning of it all, and he had agreed. When she was foolish she exasperated him, but as a successful career girl he liked her. He said she had spirit and style. He found her desirable, and although he did not say, 'I love you,' he would make love with skill and consideration.

He might have meant that marriage proposal. If he asked her again, she would marry him and go on hoping he would come to love her. But he didn't mention it again, nor did he treat her as though they were lovers. Friends, yes, host and guest, yes. No guest could have been treated better, he was with her all the time. She was entertained wonderfully. Until bedtime, of course. When bedtime came he didn't even kiss her goodnight, and she knew well enough that other nights under this roof, with other ladies, had been less platonic.

The weather stayed freezing, with no sign of a thaw, but it kept no one in. Friends and neighbours came. Each evening there were other guests around the dinner table. They came to meet the girl Orme was supposed to be marrying, although when anyone asked when he said, 'We haven't fixed a date yet,' as though the marriage was a long way away.

He doesn't like them asking that, thought Tessa. She recognised the touch of brusqueness, and no one persisted. Orme's reserve was very final. When he put up the barrier there was no way round it.

On Sunday evening there was quite a crowd, and that was when she overheard a man say, 'Not in a hurry to name the day, is he?'

'No,' said a woman, and added, 'She seems a nice girl.'

'Thank you,' thought Tessa wryly. She was a nice girl having a nice time, in this beautiful house with these people who wanted to be her friends, because they liked and admired Orme and they thought she was going to be Orme's wife.

This was her last evening here. Next morning they would have to make an early start, back to the office and the next assignment. She was wearing her long red velvet skirt and her pink silk shirt. There was colour in her cheeks—the room was warm and she had put on blusher—and her shining eyes were skilfully made up.

She thought she looked the part she was playing, especially in the mirror in the drawing room that was identical to the mirror in Orme's London

178

house. This had the same golden glow. 'Old mirrors are always kind,' Orme had said, and she thought—when the engagement ends and I hand back the ring, perhaps he might find me an old mirror out of this house so that I can hang it on the wall of my flat. Kind mirrors are hard to find.

But how could she live with a mirror from Midwinton? She would always be peering into it for reflections it had once held. Reflections of Orme.

He stood behind her now, as she glanced into the mirror and tucked a tendril of hair behind her ear, and she said, 'A matching pair—the mirrors. This one and the one in your house.'

He smiled. 'I thought you meant us.' He put an arm around her, taking her with him, and she saw Lady Ursula, sitting in a green brocade chair with a matching footstool, smiling happily at them.

Right from the moment Tessa had come downstairs on this last evening, dressed for the company they were expecting, she had felt that this was the finale. Not just the end of her weekend visit, but the end of the play. She had been acting a part ever since she went to Blackstone. A good actress lives her part, and so had Tessa. She wore Orme's ring and she was in love with Orme, but for all that it was play-acting.

The drawing room at Midwinton would have made a fantastic set for a play, and as the guests began to leave it became more and more unreal.

Tessa was a little lightheaded, although she hadn't drunk much wine. That was nervousness because she knew that if Orme said nothing more tonight, about them marrying, the odds were that they wouldn't. She hadn't expected him to make any announcements, but when everyone had gone, and they were alone here for the last time before they travelled back to London and to work, if he didn't at least repeat what he had said on Thursday night, 'Will you think about marrying me?' then she could forget it.

Her instinct told her that. When the last guests had gone she stood with Orme in the hall. Lady Ursula was leaning on her cane and on Miss Burton's arm, and as the great door closed Lady Ursula said, 'It's long past my bedtime, so I'll say goodnight.'

It wasn't very late, it was coming up to midnight, but Tessa murmured, 'We do have to make an early start, don't we, I suppose——' and that was it. Orme said goodnight to all of them, and she found herself going upstairs with Miss Burton and his grandmother.

He had made no move at all to keep her with him. He was the affable host who had said goodbye to some of the evening's guests showing more affection than he showed her. There wasn't even a token goodnight kiss for Lady Ursula's benefit, and she left Lady Ursula rather quickly on the gallery because the old lady was looking thoughtful.

Her packing for morning was done. She stripped off her clothes and her make-up, and without make-up she was pale. When she was ready for bed she stood barefoot in a white lawn nightdress, looking at the brass fourposter. She wasn't tired. But she would have to get into bed, and try to sleep, because there wasn't anything else she could do.

She hated the passive role, but what action could she take right now that she wouldn't surely regret later, except get into bed and try to sleep?

She went to the main light switch by the door, and as she touched the switch there was a knock on the door that made her jump as though she was electrocuted. Her mind shut off. She wouldn't let herself think who this might be. She slipped into her yellow towelling robe and opened the door, and it was Miss Burton holding a glass of hot milk, and Tessa let out her breath in a silent sigh of disappointment.

Miss Burton was smiling at her. 'Lady Ursula would like you to take her nightcap in for her.'

'Of course.' Tessa put on a pair of yellow mules and took the glass of milk. She would have liked to ask, 'Why?' but probably Miss Burton didn't know why, and if she did she wasn't waiting to be asked. She said, 'Goodnight again,' and went, and Tessa carried the milk and honey with a dash of whisky along to Lady Ursula's room.

The door was off the catch. As Tessa tapped Lady Ursula called, 'Come in, dear child.'

She was in bed, pillows behind her, her soft dark hair brushed loosely, her face, now without a scrap of make-up, still remarkably unlined.

'Put it on the table,' she directed, and as Tessa deposited the glass of milk she held out a hand, drawing the girl down to sit on the bed. 'I wanted to be sure of seeing you once more before you leave in the morning,' said Lady Ursula, 'I could oversleep—at my age I need my sleep. I wanted to tell you again how happy I am about this. Everything's all right, isn't it? Yes, of course it is.'

She squeezed Tessa's hand with the ring on it, and Tessa looked down at the ring. She wasn't so sure she could look straight at Orme's grandmother without giving herself away. She said, 'It's a beautiful ring. It's kind of you not to mind me wearing it.'

'You knew it was mine?' The old lady seemed surprised.

'Well—yes.'

'I didn't know that.' She smiled. 'He told me he'd given you one of my rings because it was rather sudden, and he couldn't risk you changing your mind before the shops opened.'

It wasn't true, of course, but it was as good an excuse as any. 'It was sudden,' agreed Tessa.

'I came right away to see you. The very next day.' So Orme had phoned his grandmother from Blackstone. Tessa wondered what else he had said. In spite of the hour Lady Ursula's eyes were alert rather than sleepy.

'I'm glad you approved,' Tessa said quietly.

'It wouldn't have made any difference if I hadn't.' She wasn't complaining, her tone was tolerant, telling Tessa, 'He's a very stubborn man, very like his grandfather. When he told me you were the girl he meant to marry I knew he'd made up his mind.'

That could still mean nothing. 'You are, aren't you?' said Lady Ursula.

The girl he was going to marry? 'I hope so,' said Tessa. Suppose she asked, 'How did he sound when he was telling you this? Did he say anything else? Has he said anything since?'

'I'm pleased he gave you that ring,' said Orme's grandmother, reaching for her hot milk. 'Goodnight now, my dear, and you will come back to see me soon?'

'I'd like to,' said Tessa. 'And thank you for everything.' She left her sipping her milk, and walked along the corridor, towards the gallery and her room, with her questions unasked.

If she had asked Orme's grandmother, 'Do you think he really wants to marry me?' Orme's grandmother would have said, 'But of course.' But the

182

only one who could answer that question was Orme.

At her bedroom door Tessa stood still for a few seconds. Lights were still on below. If he was down there she could say, 'I can't sleep, I've come for a book.' But she wouldn't have to go seeking Orme to get a book. Whatever she decided to say would probably come out differently, so she would find him first, and then somehow she would ask him where they went from here.

'Wear your ring a little longer,' he had said on Thursday night, 'and if you find you're getting used to it I should be honoured and delighted to discuss how we might proceed from there.'

He hadn't shown much passion nor much impatience, but it was Sunday night now. She had worn the ring for three more days and she *was* used to it, and there was no time like the present for discussing the future.

She walked slowly down the stairs, very much in two minds about this. Her common sense told her she was a fool rushing in, that no one pushed Orme, that if she showed she was over-eager he might decide she was not after all the kind of wife he wanted.

But for all that her feet kept going. It was quiet here, although the big chandelier was still on. She went to the study, he might be getting papers together for work, but he wasn't there. No one seemed to be about, and she was making no sound in her soft-soled slippers.

Perhaps everyone had gone to bed, and forgotten to switch off the chandelier, and she would have to wait till morning. She couldn't knock on bedroom doors, at least she didn't think she could. But she *had* to talk to him, and when she opened the door of the small parlour and he was sitting there it was almost a relief to see him.

There was a side lamp burning, and a glow of fire embers, and as she stepped into the room Orme and the two dogs got up together. 'What is it?' Orme asked.

He probably thought she had forgotten something, like her handbag. She had forgotten how she was going to lead up to this discussion she wanted. She gulped and blurted, 'Suppose I said I'd marry you right away?'

'Will you?' He didn't say, 'Hold on now, not so fast,' and in for a penny in for a pound, Tessa gulped again and asked,

'Do you love me?'

'Of course.' But he made no move towards her and she said,

'There's no of course about it. You never said so.'

'Why should I ask you to marry me if I didn't love you?'

The clock ticked. She had listened to it ticking just before Lady Ursula spoke of disinheriting Orme, and she said quietly, 'I thought perhaps to keep me wearing the ring. To keep your grandmother happy. For Midwinton. In case she left it to someone else.'

'What in heaven's name gave you that idea?' He sounded as though it was laughable, and perhaps it was, but it was what she had been told.

She said, 'Your grandmother told me she'd threatened to disinherit you unless you found her a nice granddaughter,' and Orme did laugh then.

'So she does,' he said. 'Constantly. That's one of her little jokes. She's very comfortably off, but the house and the estate are mine, and she knows it doesn't matter to me where she leaves her money.'

Before Tessa had had time for that to sink in he asked, 'Do you like the house?'

'Of course,' she answered automatically, her mind whirling.

'Good,' he said. 'That's why I brought you here this weekend. I hoped that after you'd seen Midwinton perhaps you'd take us both on.'

She could feel her eyes getting wider. She heard herself croak, 'You really want to marry me?' Not for Midwinton. For herself. He wanted Tessa Harris, and she wasn't dreaming.

'How many times do you need telling?' He still didn't sound like a lover. He sounded more than ever like he did at work, when someone was being thick and he couldn't get the message into their head. 'I want to marry you. I'm going to marry you. At once would suit me best, but if you need time to get over Paul Mellor and used to the idea of marrying me time you shall have.'

'Who says I need time?' she shrieked at him. 'I never asked you to be patient.'

For a split second longer they glared at each other. Then Orme said, 'Tessa?' in a strange choking voice, and she ran to him and he held his arms wide and drew her against him, suffocatingly close.

She could feel his body shaking, she was trembling herself as his lips brushed her forehead and then her mouth. Her lips parted and they kissed long and hungrily, with a passion that would have left her reeling if she hadn't had him to cling to.

When the kissing stopped he still held her tight, then he lifted her, carrying her to the sofa. The mules slipped from her feet, her bare toes looked white in the soft glow of lamplight and dying fire, and she lay with her head on his shoulder. She rubbed her chin against the velvet jacket and said, 'This is nice.'

'Very nice.' He bowed his head, breathing in the faint perfume of her hair.

She could still hardly believe it, but she wasn't questioning it any more. Well, not questioning, just wondering. It was something to wonder at. 'It's sudden, isn't it?' she said. She touched the ring on her finger. 'When did you—want this to be for real?'

He took her hand and held it, covered by his own much larger hand. 'When I saw you wearing that ring you'd bought yourself,' he told her, 'I couldn't ask you about it. I thought it knocked me back because if you were marrying you might leave your job and I didn't want to lose you from the team. I came round to your flat that night to try to talk you out of it somehow, anyhow.

'Then you told me about Paul Mellor and I made up my mind he wasn't taking you away whatever I had to do to stop him.'

That much she knew. She waited and he said, 'It was a pretty ring, but I couldn't stand it on your hand. You had to wear my ring. And when I took you to the Mellors' that first night it was because I had to see my enemy.'

She said incredulously, 'You were jealous of *Paul*?'

'Oh yes.' The deep voice admitted no doubt on that. 'I could cheerfully have killed him that night, although I was still telling myself it was because he might persuade you to give up your job.' He grinned wryly at his own self-deception. 'Then, as we drove away, you talked about the letters you wrote to him. A lot of letters, you said, and I knew that I wanted your letters, your love letters, because I was in love with you.' The deep voice was husky now.

'Never before like this,' he said. 'Never again for me. Not anyone else.'

He looked deep into her eyes and he was vulnerable now, holding nothing back. This was the naked look of love. 'I thought you might still care for Mellor,' he said, 'that was why I daren't rush you. I would have waited, but waiting would have been the hardest thing I ever had to do.'

She touched his cheek gently. 'Paul was an infatuation. I know the difference now.'

Paul was the shadow, and Orme was so real. 'When you kissed me,' she said, 'in Blackstone, the only time you kissed me till now'—he had told her to stop dreaming, she had thought he was angry with her—'what would have happened if I'd kissed you back?'

She had come within a hair's breath of doing that, and he chuckled. 'If you had I couldn't have let you go. As it was I nearly didn't, that was why I daren't risk it again.'

He was smiling at her, but as he held her against him she knew that he meant every word he said. 'I don't know how it would affect you if I made love to you, but I sure as hell know what it would do to me, and I wasn't sure you were prepared to take on a man who couldn't bear to let you out of his sight.'

'But I am,' she teased tenderly. 'So long as sometimes he'd settle for letters!'

'Not often?'

'Oh no.'

She could feel his breath, light and very warm on her cheek, and the comforting thrilling strength of his arm around her. 'Will you marry me next week?' He waited for her answer, and she knew that he held his breath.

'Of course.' She smiled up at him. 'But about

these great-grandchildren——'

'In our good time, not hers. She'll live to be a hundred.'

That was quite likely, and that would be lovely. 'I'm glad she likes me,' said Tessa. 'But she said it would have been all the same if she hadn't, because you're a very stubborn man.'

'Don't believe her.' It was true and they both knew it, and that there would always be arguments, but that neither would hurt the other. Orme asked quietly, 'Did she tell you what else I said when I phoned her?'

'That you meant to marry me.'

'And that I loved you very much more than you loved me.'

Possibly, then. She had been walking with Paul over the hills when Orme made that phone call from the Stag's Head. She had known that Orme disturbed her, but she had not realised then that she loved him.

She said slowly, 'If you do it must be a powerful loving. I can't imagine anything stronger than the way I feel about you.'

'Can't you?' His hands moved beneath the towelling robe she wore, on to her bare shoulders, drawing her closer still. Then he began to kiss her and she knew that he was right. Their loving was just beginning.

THE KING'S SHADOW
Judith Polley

The turbulent days of the Civil War . . . . Katherine Ashley's path is crossed constantly by the King's Shadow and she is caught up in a web of intrigue, blackmail and suspense.

THE FORTUNE-HUNTER
Julia Herbert

Poole Harbour in Georgian times was the smuggling centre of the south coast of England. Against this sinister background, the popular author of THE RUNAWAYS has set a fast-moving, exciting romance.

PURITAN WIFE
Elizabeth de Guise

Constance, a young Puritan orphan, finds her beautiful ancestral home suddenly bestowed on the Royalist Earl of Brede by his grateful sovereign Charles II. Left homeless so dramatically, her only solution is to marry the magnificent Earl, but love him — how can she?

FRANCESCA
Valentina Luellen

Italy in the sixteenth century when the notorious Borgias ruled. Francesca, compelled to marry into the family in order to save her brother's life, finds herself surrounded by treachery and her own life in danger.

Four more exciting titles in our

Masquerade Series

Available October 1977

50p each

Forthcoming Mills & Boon Romances

FLY BEYOND THE SUNSET *by Anne Hampson*
Faun was a perfectly competent airline pilot — so why, when
she crash-landed in the Borneo jungle, did Clive Tarrant
have to be on board to make things worse?

FLAMINGO MOON *by Margaret Pargeter*
When Eve arrived at Raoul DuBare's house in the Camargue,
he threw her out literally. But Eve came back . . . .

THE LION OF QUIMERA *by Amanda Doyle*
Teresa thought she had applied for a governess's job in Spain,
so how had she ended up on Quimera, off the South
American coast, and tyrannised over by an imposing Marques?

PINEAPPLE GIRL *by Betty Neels*
A grateful patient gave Eloise a pineapple, which she promptly
dropped at Timon van Zeilst's feet — and lost her heart at
the same time!

PORTRAIT OF JAIME *by Margaret Way*
Jaime's grandfather, whom she have never seen, had sent for
her. But if she went, she would be in Quinn Sterling's
power . . . .

A TRIAL MARRIAGE *by Anne Mather*
Rachel was eighteen and Jake twenty years older — rich,
sophisticated, cynical. Could they ever by happy together?

THE WRONG MAN TO LOVE *by Roberta Leigh*
Samantha's inheritance brought her nothing but disaster, for
because of it she met Zachary Farrell — and he had no time
for her at all!

TEMPLE OF THE MOON *by Sara Craven*
A trip to Yucatan should have solved all Gabrielle's problems,
but instead she encountered a new one; the disturbing
Shaun Lennox . . . .

ACROSS A CROWDED ROOM *by Lilian Peake*
Only one man — Rosco Hamden — could save Lisette from
disaster. But could she pay his price?

FRASER'S BRIDE *by Elizabeth Graham*
Everyone said Lara would make the perfect wife for Jerry.
But she fell in love with his brother Matt, who didn't want
her!

Available November 1977 — Only 40p each

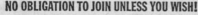